THE
NO-GOOD NINE

THE NO-GOOD NINE

JOHN BEMELMANS MARCIANO

VIKING

VIKING

An imprint of Penguin Random House LLC

375 Hudson Street

New York, New York 10014

First published in the United States of America by Viking,
an imprint of Penguin Random House LLC, 2018

Copyright © 2018 by John Bemelmans Marciano
Interior illustration copyright © 2018 by Rebecca Mock

LIBRARY OF CONGRESS CATALOGING-IN-PUBLICATION DATA
Names: Marciano, John Bemelmans, author.
Title: The No-Good Nine / by John Bemelmans Marciano.
Description: New York : Viking, [2018]. | Summary: In 1931, nine naughty
children who received coal in their stockings travel from Pittsburgh
to the North Pole to plead their case to Santa Claus. |
Identifiers: LCCN 2018000523 (print) | LCCN 2018008039 (ebook) | ISBN
9781101997864 (ebook) | ISBN 9781101997840 (hardback)
Subjects: | CYAC: Behavior—Fiction. | Adventure and adventurers—Fiction. |
Santa Claus—Fiction. | Christmas—Fiction. | Depressions—1929—Fiction.
| United States—History—1919–1933—Fiction. | Humorous stories. | BISAC:
JUVENILE FICTION / Action & Adventure / General. | JUVENILE FICTION /
Humorous Stories. | JUVENILE FICTION / Social Issues / Runaways.
Classification: LCC PZ7.M328556 (ebook) | LCC PZ7.M328556 No 2018 (print) |
DDC [Fic]—dc23 | LC record available at https://lccn.loc.gov/2018000523

Printed in U.S.A.   Book design by Nancy Brennan

1   3   5   7   9   10   8   6   4   2

TO THE SO-GOOD READERS
OF RED HOOK:

*Pearl, Thea, Nathan, Jasper,
Oliver, Odette, Imogen,
Cy, and Galatea*

—◆—

THE
NO-GOOD NINE

PART ONE

The Secret Origin of the No-Good Nine

You've heard of how bad kids get coal in their Christmas stockings, right? You may think it's a hollow threat, but it really used to happen. And then it stopped. In 1932, if you want to be exact.

Why did it stop, you ask? It stopped because of **us**.

The No-Good Nine!

Maybe you know how we tangled with Tarzan and journeyed to Oz. Or how we fought alongside Buck Rogers in the future and rescued Sherlock Holmes in the Wild West. And how we might—or might not!—have discovered Atlantis.

What you don't know is how we got together in the first place. You *can't* know it, because our origin story has been a matter of top-level international security for almost a century. But now—finally—the records can be unsealed, and you can know the true story of how we changed Christmas forever.

But before we became the No-Good Nine, we were just nine regular kids.

Well, sort of regular.

EPISODE ONE:
MEET THE NO-GOOD NINE

1. THE KNOW-IT-ALL

It was nearly the end of 1931, an out-and-out lousy year. In fact, it might have been the worst year ever.

The Great Depression was in full swing, and it wasn't called that because everyone was depressed. (Although that was true, too.) It was the Great Depression because nobody had any money or a job. Nearly nobody, anyway.

The newspapers were filled with stories of people jumping off buildings and hoboes riding train cars, but today was the day when no one was supposed to worry about stuff like that. Because today was Christmas, the best day of the year! Right?

Wrong!

Wrong, in particular, for the Know-It-All. It was right before dawn when the Know-It-All—or Peter, as he would still be called for a few more days—woke up with that amazing feeling you get once a year. When your first thought is: *It's Christmas!*

He shook his sister awake and they crept down the creaky stairs together.

"Santa was *here*!" Peter's little sister screeched.

"Of course he was h-h-here. It's Christmas," Peter said, in that know-it-all-y way of his, which had to be as annoying to his little sister as it was to the rest of us.

In the living room, two stockings were hanging over the fireplace. The one marked BETSY was lumpy, packed, and overflowing. The one marked PETER looked different.

As in empty.

Stunned—worried—confused—Peter quickly ran through all the things on his Christmas list, which is reproduced below for your convenience.

September 1, 1931
Sewickley, Penn.

Dear Mr. Santa Claus,

Firstly, I would like to thank you for all the gifts you have given me in the past. Most especially I'd like to thank you for last year, when I asked for more presents than ever and you managed to get me every single one. I truly appreciate it.

I would also like you to know that I would completely understand if this year, which has been so bad for so many children, you were not able to entirely fulfill my wishes. I'll be happy and grateful for whatever you are able to give me. After all, I am one of the lucky kids whose father still has a job, a fact for which I am thankful every single day.

As for my list, I would like:

An Erector set
Lincoln Logs
A Lionel Train
One novel, preferably <u>Tarzan at the Earth's Core</u>
One pulp magazine subscription, preferably
  <u>Amazing Stories</u>
<u>Funk and Wagnalls New Standard Encyclopedia</u>
A new compass
and
Fruit

As ever, thank you, Mr. Claus, and thanks also to your entire staff of elves who do such excellent work, year in and year out.

Yours sincerely,
Peter Czaplynsky

Why any kid would want an encyclopedia for Christmas, I have no clue. But that was the Know-It-All for you. He wanted to *know* it *all*.

But right now Peter was regretting his letter. Maybe he shouldn't have been so quick to tell Santa it was O.K.

to take care of the less fortunate kids and not him.

"There *is* a lump in the toe," his little sister said, feeling at the stocking. "Something *is* in here!"

But he hadn't asked for anything that small. Unless it was—*groan*—the fruit! Why did he even bother asking for that, anyway?

Peter turned over his stocking. What was stuck in the toe was something far worse than fruit.

It was **coal**.

The horrible truth hit Peter like a punch to the stomach:

He had been put on Santa's Naughty List!

How could this be? Peter thought. There must be some kind of mistake!

When Peter's parents came down, Betsy couldn't contain herself.

"Santa brought Peter coal! Santa brought Peter coal!" she said, jumping up and down. "And I got everything I wanted!! Peter's NAUGHTY and I'm NICE!"

"How can that be?" Peter's father said.

"There must be some kind of mistake!" Peter's mother said.

After all, Peter had been a good boy all year long, the same as ever. Betsy, on the other hand, spent half of first grade sitting in the corner with a dunce cap on or getting the back of her hand slapped with a ruler. (Yeah, that stuff *really* happened in 1931.)

Peter felt sick all that day, like the hurt of that punch just wouldn't go away. Even at Christmas dinner at Grandma's with his cousins, he couldn't be happy.

And it wasn't just because he didn't get any presents. It was because he was so *ashamed*.

That night there was no getting to sleep. Everyone was so sure it was a mistake. What if it really was? Couldn't Santa make a mistake? After all, everyone makes mistakes. And when you make a mistake, you try to fix it, right? So Peter snuck back downstairs to see if Santa had come back to deliver his presents.

He had not.

Peter started looking under furniture and behind the stacked wood to see if there was any place a present could've gotten left by accident, until the only place to look was in the heap of ashes in the fireplace. Maybe something had fallen out of Santa's bag when he was coming down the chimney?

Peter got on his hands and knees and started searching through the cinders. It was a desperate act, not to mention a dirty one. And that was when he found it.

No, not a present.

A *list*.

It was burned at the edges and half covered in soot. At first, Peter thought it was one of his mom's shopping lists. But the handwriting wasn't hers—it was in some kind of fancy script.

He looked more closely at the paper. It was a list of *kids*. On the page were their names, ages, and addresses, along with a nasty-sounding description of each. *Thief, Brat, Biter, Cruel, Bully, Liar,* and so on.

Boy, you wouldn't want to be called any of the things on *this* list. This was a list of really bad kids.

Then at the bottom of the page, he saw his own name.

Peter Czaplynsky, 12, **KNOW-IT-ALL**
1028 Thorn Street

Finally it hit him—like he was ten pins and this burnt piece of paper was a bowling ball hurtling at him.

This *list*—this was Santa's list.

THE NAUGHTY LIST!

And it was this list that led Peter to **me**.

2. ME

It was the morning after Christmas. I was throwing snowballs on the sidewalk outside my house, trying to knock the head off a snowman some little kids in the neighborhood had built. I reared back and

BAP!

I knocked the carrot off its face. *Jake!*

(Back in 1931, "jake" meant cool.)

Making another snowball, I saw him walking up the

street—Peter. He was looking up and down from a piece of paper, and checking out the building number on my house. He looked confused, like he was lost. But how could he be lost? He lived three streets away.

"Hey!" I called. "Whattya standin' there lookin' stupid for?"

I knew Peter, although I wouldn't say we were friends. At least not yet. We were in the same sixth-grade class—sort of.

("Sort of" because I didn't much go to school. More on *that* later.)

Peter looked down to his piece of paper again, and said, "I didn't know your n-n-name was Luigi!"

"It's not," I said.

"Are you l-l-lying, Looie?"

"No, I'm not lying. My name is Lewis," I said, throwing the snowball. I knocked out the snowman's corncob pipe. "Who told you it was Luigi?"

"Did you get c-c-coal in your stocking at Christmas?" he asked.

"No, of course not!" I told him Santa gave me the Erector set I'd been wanting all year and how jake it was.

Peter asked if we could play with it, but I told him I had let my cousin Tony borrow it. "He loves buildin' stuff."

"You're lying," Peter said.

"*Prove* it," I said.

He held out the piece of paper he'd been staring at. It was half burned.

"What's that?" I said, suspicious.

"It's Santa's N-N-Naughty List," Peter said.

"Wow, gimme that!" I said, and ripped the page out of Peter's hands.

"G-g-give it back!" he said.

"This is so *swell*!" I said, using another word that meant cool back then. "Hey, look, here's my name—Luigi Curidi!"

"I thought you said your name *wasn't* Luigi," Peter said. "But I g-g-guess I shouldn't be surprised, LIAR!" He pointed at the word right next to my name.

Luigi Curidi, 12, LIAR

It was a fair description. I *was* a liar. For instance, I had lied to Peter about practically everything I had said.

Santa had *not* given me an Erector set, and if he had, I certainly wouldn't have lent it to my jerky cousin Tony. I *had* gotten coal in my stocking. But unlike with Peter, it was no surprise. I always got coal in my stocking. (Even so, I kept putting up a stocking every year. I too hoped that Santa made an occasional mistake.)

"Hey, look!" I said, pointing further down the list. "Here *you* are!"

"I know," he said miserably.

"And it says you're a know-it-all! Wow," I said, "Santa's really good at this! You *are* a know-it-all!"

The Know-It-All—as I would forever after call the boy formerly known as Peter—looked annoyed and snatched the list back from me.

I asked if he wanted to do something fun. Go sledding? Build an igloo? Have a snowball fight? But he didn't.

He was obsessed with The List.

"This list is too important!" he said. "We can't l-l-let it go to waste. It's been dropped on us for a reason!"

I pointed out that it wasn't much of a list—just one lousy page of a much bigger list. A *book* of lists. And even at that, there were only about thirty or so names you could make out. The rest were all too burnt to read.

"Well, it's not fair!" the Know-It-All said. "Having a list like this is an injustice! It's t-t-t-terrible to give some kids exactly what they want for Christmas and give other ones coal."

I shrugged. I always got coal and I *was* a liar, so I didn't know how unfair it was. "Besides, I didn't hear you complaining when Santa was giving *you* everything you wanted."

The Know-It-All ignored me. "We have to do something about this!"

"But what can we do?" I said.

As it wound up, the Know-It-All had an idea of exactly what we could do.

A BIG idea.

But I didn't know that—yet.

3. THE BRAT

It was a long walk from where the Know-It-All and I lived up to Sewickley Heights, the rich part of town. And when I'm talking rich, I'm talking *millionaire* rich. This is where the Pittsburghers who had made truckloads of money with steel factories and coal mining and the railroads came to live. And boy, did these millionaires like to live in big houses.

In fact, you couldn't call even them houses. They were castles, with big stone walls surrounding them.

Walking up here, I started to get nervous. Some poor and dirty Italian kid like me could get arrested just for breathing the same air as these people. I wasn't even an American citizen yet. What if I got deported back to Italy? I didn't know how to speak Italian!

"What are we doing here again?" I asked the Know-It-All.

"Meeting one of the other kids on the l-l-list," he said.

The first part of the Know-It-All's big idea was to

go around and talk to other Naughty Listers. But as far as I knew, that was *all* we were doing.

"And *why* do we want to go around meeting a bunch of rotten kids?" I asked.

"How do you know they're so r-r-rotten?" he said. "We're on the l-l-list, too."

"Yeah, but for nothin' dangerous," I said. The other kids on the list were cheats, thieves, bullies, and hooligans. One kid—with the crazy name Tuesday—was labeled CRUEL. "We might get ourselves killed!"

"Well, the one who l-l-lives up here is the Brat," the Know-It-All said. "That doesn't sound too d-d-d-d-dangerous."

It didn't sound like my new best friend, either.

Henry Alistair Chaudfront III, 12, BRAT

When we got to the Brat's address, it wound up he lived in the biggest, fanciest mansion of them all. It had a tower and iron gates twelve feet tall that led into the driveway. About the only thing it didn't have was a moat and a drawbridge. Looking at it, I couldn't blame Henry Chaudfront III for being a brat. If I lived here, I'd have been a brat too.

While the Know-It-All double-checked the name and address, someone yelled, "**Hey!** What are you kids doing out there?"

My heart jumped and I looked over to see a man in a yellow uniform walking toward us on the other side of the gate. He must have been a servant.

I wanted to run, but the Know-It-All said, "We're l-l-looking for Henry!"

"You mean Sparky?" the yellow-uniformed man said.

"Yeah, *Sparky*," I said. "We're pals of his. Good ol' Sparky!"

The guy squinted.

"Sparky's a monster," he said. "And Sparky doesn't have friends."

But he went to go get him anyway.

"Are you *sure* we want to do this?" I said.

The kid who came out was like no kid I'd ever seen before, except maybe in a movie. He looked like a miniature adult, with a flap of slicked-back hair and a bow tie around his neck.

What kind of kid wears a *tie*?

The Brat looked the both of us up and down like we were gum that might get stuck to the bottom of his shoe.

"What do you two hoodlums want?" he said.

The Know-It-All explained what had happened. Sort of. He wasn't the best explainer when he was nervous. For one thing, there was that stutter. For another, he had trouble getting to the point. Or maybe it was just that his point didn't seem like the point. He kept talking about how unfair it was that some kids got presents and others didn't.

"Well, I get lots of presents," the Brat said.

"Yeah, the ones your parents *bought* for you," I said.

"Free presents are for poor people," he said. "My family doesn't need some fat old elf's charity."

The Know-It-All then brought out the list. He pointed to the name *Henry Alistair Chaudfront III* and then to his Naughty Crime—BRAT.

What happened next, you wouldn't believe unless you saw it. (And boy, would I see it a *lot* over the years.)

The Brat got mad. But not mad like how normal people get mad. With him, it was like sticking a thermometer in a pot of boiling water and watching the mercury rise until it exploded.

His face changed colors. It went from pink to red to dark red to something darker than dark red. And it wasn't just one part of his face, like his cheeks or his ears. It was his entire head.

Well, except for his eyeballs. Those just looked like they were going to pop out of his skull.

"We have to **do** something about this!" he said.

"Yes, we d-d-do!" the Know-It-All said. "We have a plan!"

"We do?" I said.

"Yes, we d-d-**do**," the Know-It-All said. "And the plan is to go to Santa's workshop."

"Wait, to *what?*" I said.

He wanted to *go* to Santa's? That was totally ridiculous! Except the Know-It-All, with his know-it-all-ness, had figured out how to get there.

Or so he claimed.

He said we had to take a train to Quebec, where we would switch to a boat that would take us up the Saint Lawrence River. Once we got to the sea, we'd switch to a different boat that would take us to a magical lighthouse where there existed some kind of ferry service to Santa's workshop.

Thinking back on it, it sounds like a really stupid plan. What I *should* have done was walk back home and never talk to either of these two Naughty Listers again.

But right then the plan sounded pretty swell.

And to the Brat?

"That's genius!" he said. "We go to that grubby old elf's factory and we break all the toys of the nice kids of the world!"

"Can't we play with them first?" I said. "The toys, I mean."

"Good idea!" the Brat said. "We play with them and then we break them and *then* we go to Santa and show him what we think of him and his rotten list!"

"That's the part I w-w-want to talk about," the Know-It-All said, and fumbled to take out a notebook.

"I've been working on a sternly w-w-worded petition to read to Santa about the unfairness of the Naughty List," he said. "About its lack of democratic principles, and the v-v-violation of *habeas corpus* and—"

"Hay-bee-is *whats*-is?" I said.

"Forget the fancy words," the Brat said. "The only thing we need to give that stupid old elf is a punch in his big, fat stomach."

"But the p-p-p-petition," the Know-It-All said, holding up his marbled composition book.

"Oh fine," the Brat said, rolling his eyes. "You read your petition, and *then* I'll punch him in his stomach."

There was one problem. All these train and boat tickets were going to cost a lot of money. But that wound up not being a problem at all, because the Brat offered to pay our way.

"So . . . is this gonna be like a club?" I said.

I had always wanted to be in a club. A *secret* club. The kind with special code names and secret handshakes and stuff. And a password.

"*Ice bucket!*" I said.

"What?" the Brat said.

"*Ice bucket!*" I repeated. "That can be our secret password."

"That's the dumbest thing I ever heard," he said.

But it was decided. We were forming a secret society

of Naughty Listers, with the aim of going to Santa's and playing with the toys of the nice kids of the world.

And the next day, we would go in search of members.

4. THE NEXT DAY

It was early, and the Know-It-All and I were walking to the meeting place. We had both been busy.

The Know-It-All had spent half the night going through the list and plotting the addresses of each of the other kids on a map of Pittsburgh, which was where the rest of the Naughty Listers lived.

Our particular page of the Naughty List covered only the greater Pittsburgh area and only kids with last names starting Ce to Cz. The whole of the Naughty List had to be huge!

"Extrapolating from population size and the relative alphabetical distribution of these names," the Know-It-All said, "I calculate that the complete Naughty List contains approximately 328,453 children in the United States alone."

Which is a whole lot of horrible kids.

But we weren't looking to recruit *all* of them, not even all the ones on our single page. We just wanted kids our own age—give or take a year—and nobody who had committed any actual crimes. That meant no Pickpocket, no

Shoplifter, no Robber, and no Murderer. Yes, there really *was* a murderer on the list. I'm not lying!*

Oh yeah—and no girls.

This all narrowed the list considerably.

When we got to the old abandoned icehouse on the edge of town, there was no sign of the Brat. It was his idea to meet here, although I wasn't sure why. To get to Pittsburgh, I usually just hopped the train. If you hid in the bathroom long enough, the conductor could never check your ticket.

Mr. Richer-than-Rich said he'd see to us getting into the city some other way. Even so, it never occurred to me he might be driving the car that came rumbling up. This was because of what kind of car it was—a Doozy. Literally.

(*Doozy* was the nickname for a Duesenberg, a long, open car so amazing that anything amazing came to be called a doozy.)

Of course, I couldn't see who it was, since the driver's face was covered in a racing cap, goggles, and a scarf.

"What's the password?" I asked.

"It's me, stupid," the Brat said, taking off his goggles.

That was a really good password. Much better than *ice bucket*. "O.K., forget the old password," I said. "The new password is *It's me, stupid!*"

"How can you be driving!" the Know-It-All said. "You're not old enough to d-d-drive!"

*He's lying. —The Editor

"But I *am* rich," the Brat said. "Which makes me old enough to do whatever I want."

The Know-It-All felt the same rules should apply to everyone. The Brat agreed—so long as it was everyone *else*.

All I cared about was I was going to get to ride in a Doozy!

"Take your filthy shoes off before you come in the car, you twit!" the Brat said.

He grinded the Doozy into gear, jammed on the gas, and kicked up dirt and snow under the back wheels as we sped off.

With the way the Brat was driving, it looked like the Know-It-All was going to barf.

Me, I *loved* it.

"This is so great!" I shouted above the car noise. "The first official mission of the Secret Society of He-Man Naughty Listers is under way!"

"We are **not** calling ourselves the Secret Society of He-Man Naughty Listers!" the Brat shouted back.

"He's right!" the Know-It-All yelled from the back. "That is a *d-d-dumb* name!"

But we *had* to call ourselves that, because the name was already on the invitations.

This was what *I* had been busy with.

YOU ARE INVITED TO THE FIRST
OFFICIAL MEETING

of
THE SECRET SOCIETY OF HE-MAN
NAUGHTY LISTERS
at
THE UNITED PITTSBURGH MUNITIONS
FACTORY
at
HIGH NOON, DECEMBER 28, 1931
::

TELL NO ONE!

It looked darn good, I thought. Almost like a professional invite.

"This l-l-looks like it was scratched out by a chicken," the Know-It-All said.

"A *dimwitted chicken*," the Brat said. "With its left claw."

I snatched the invites back. No one understands a true artist.

Pittsburgh was about fifteen miles away, and we were getting close. You could tell because everything was beginning to turn black. The snow on the ground, the houses—all black. As we got farther in, the air itself became a black fog, and the street lamps were on, even though it was the middle of the morning. And you know why everything was black?

Coal!

Coal wasn't just for stockings in 1931. Coal powered pretty much everything in Pittsburgh, a city that had two nicknames: *Steel City* and *Hell with the Lid Off.* The first was because of all the factories; the second because Pittsburgh was so polluted, the rivers occasionally caught on fire.

The first kid we went to see was:

Sammy Cemolian, 11, BULLY

The Bully lived in a row of small, shabby houses separated by narrow alleys. The Know-It-All and I got out of the car, but the Brat didn't want to leave the Doozy alone in such an unsavory-looking area.

I knocked on the Bully's door. And kept knocking.

"Y'uns are gonna have to knock a whole lot louder if y'uns arc lookin' for Cemolians!" said a plump lady pinning laundry out a second-story window in the alley. "They left this morning for Scranton. Relatives or sump'm."

Strike one.

The next kid on the map was:

Ronnie Chickles, 13, FIREBUG

The Firebug lived just a few streets away and he *was* home.

Unfortunately.

"Should we really be recruiting an a-a-a-*arsonist*?"

the Know-It-All said as we rang the doorbell.

A minute later, a gangly, weird-looking kid with red hair opened the door.

"What *is* it?" he said angrily.

He had a crazy look, with wide-open eyes that didn't blink.

The Know-It-All opened his mouth, but nothing came out. It was like he was stuttering on silence.

"What are *you* lookin' at?" the Firebug said, turning his crazy no-blink eyes on me.

"The address!" I said, pointing at the house number. "It's the wrong one!"

We both turned tail and ran back to the Doozy.

Strike two.

We hoped to have more luck with:

Tommy Crank, 12, HOOLIGAN

"This time, *I'll* do the talking," the Brat said, parking. "Which one of you wants to stay with the Doozy?"

"Me!" I said, raising my hand. "Me, me, me, me, **me!**"

"Have you ever driven a car before?" the Brat said.

"Sure I have," I said. "Lotsa times."

"Well, *don't!*" the Brat said. "Drive, that is. And don't let anyone touch the car. Or look at it!"

The Hooligan lived in an apartment building, but most of the names next to the buzzers were crossed out or missing. There was no *Crank* anywhere.

"Who y'uns lookin' fer?" said a teenager hanging around outside. He was smoking.

The Brat asked if he knew who Tommy Crank was.

"Sure, I know Tommy Crank. Who doesn't? The Crank boys is famous. You know that gang the Mug Uglies? Tommy's brother Jimmy is the one 'at started it." The kid blew smoke in their faces. "He's in jail now. They say he might get the Big Chair."

"The B-B-B-Big Chair?" the Know-It-All said.

"Yeah, you know, the **Big Chair**, the hot squat. **BZZT!**"

The teenager shook his whole body like he was getting electrocuted and then went limp. Smoke started twirling out of his nostrils. Then he opened his eyes, laughed, and yelled down the street.

"Hey, Tommy! These fellers is lookin' for you!"

At the corner were three kids—if you could even call them kids. One of them had a mustache.

"Oh yeah? Who's they?" the biggest kid said.

This was the Hooligan.

The Hooligan and the other two were making snow grenades. Snow grenades were snowballs that were dipped in a pail of water and left out to freeze. They didn't just hurt when you got hit by one—they could put you in the hospital.

But neither the snow grenades nor the size of the

Hooligan intimidated the Brat, who went right up and told Crank about finding the Naughty List, putting together a secret society, and having a meeting.

I couldn't believe how brave he was.

Or how dumb.

The whole time the Brat talked, the Hooligan looked stupefied. Then the Brat handed him one of the invites and the Hooligan read it. He had to move his lips while he did, but once he was done, he burst into laughter.

"What's this? An invitation to a little baby-*aby* tea party? Aw, that's so cute! Lookit these cute baby-*aby* boys with their baby-*aby* club," the Hooligan said to his friends, who were competing for who could laugh the loudest.

And that was when the thing with the Brat's face happened again—when it turned all purply red like a bunch of smashed raspberries. "Stop making **fun** of me, you crumby hoodlum *fink*!"

The Hooligan's face went straight from laughing to furious. He shoved the Brat hard to the ground.

"You little babies tryin' to start a gang?" he said. "Well, say hello to a *real* gang—the Mug Uglies!"

The Know-It-All picked the Brat up off the sidewalk and whistled as loud as he could.

"Looie!" the Know-It-All called to me, waving. "B-b-bring the car!"

I turned the Doozy on and tried to put the stick into gear, but it stalled out. Darn! How did this thing work?

Meanwhile, the Hooligan and his pals were laughing as the Know-It-All tried to drag away the Brat, who kept screaming to be unhanded.

"Let me at them!" he shouted. "That wasn't fair! He caught me when I wasn't looking. Put up your dukes! Let's settle this like real men!"

The Hooligan mocked him, waving his fists up in the air like in one of those old boxing photos. "Yes, let's put up our *dukes*," he said in a fake snooty accent. The other Mug Uglies hooted with laughter.

"Looie!" the Know-It-All hollered. "The **car**!"

I was trying! But every time I put the Doozy in gear and stepped on the gas, it jerked forward and stalled out. I kept gunning the engine and stalling, gunning and stalling.

"I thought you knew how to d-d-drive!" the Know-It-All yelled.

"I lied!" I said, just as I finally got the thing moving forward in a herk and a jerk.

"The car!" the Brat said, suddenly forgetting about the insults. He ran toward the Doozy.

"Hey, don't let 'em get away!" the Hooligan yelled, and hurled a snow grenade at the Brat. It plugged him square in the back of the head, knocking his big flap of pomaded hair loose so it fell over his eyes. A couple more whistled by—I was ducking my head under the dash—and then one nailed the Know-It-All in the butt.

"Ow!" he yelped.

By now, the two of them had reached the Doozy, which was rolling forward with a horrible screech. The Brat opened the driver's-side door and pushed me out of the way. "Haven't you heard of second gear?" he said.

Oh, right! *Second* gear!

The Know-It-All leapt over the side and into the back.

A snow grenade just barely missed the windshield as the Brat swerved the car around in a U-turn, and he jammed it into third gear. The Mug Uglies were running after us, hurling their snow bombs. One nailed the trunk, denting it.

"No!" the Brat yelled.

Strike three.

◆ ◆ ◆

We retired to the nearest soda shop to think out our options.

"Maybe we need to be a little more choosy," the Know-It-All said.

"Ya *think*?" I said, and slurped loudly on a straw.

"I could have taken that Hooligan," the Brat said,

brushing his black hair flap back into place—again. "Him *and* his gang."

"Yeah, you and your army of servants, maybe," I said.

The Brat wanted to forget about finding any more members, but the Know-It-All insisted on finishing the list. The Brat thought it should be *his* choice, since he was the one paying for everybody's tickets, while the Know-It-All believed it should be *his* choice, since he was the one who had found the list and knew how to get to Santa's.

"Hey, guys, how about this one?" I said, pointing to:

Billy Cunkel, 12, LAZY

"At least he should be easy to run away from."

Which wound up being true.

We found the Lazy lying in his room, staring at the wall. Which, apparently, was pretty much all he ever did.

However, he did accept our invitation without looking like he wanted to kill us. (Or actually trying to.)

"Well, that's *one* recruit," I said when we got back into the Doozy.

The other two looked at me like I was nuts.

But what was nuts was who were going to meet next.

The Cruel!

5. THE CRUEL

The Brat was the only one who wanted to recruit:

Tuesday Commons, 13, CRUEL

"This sounds like just the kind of guy we need to go face Santa," the Brat said.

"But how c-c-c-cruel is he?" the Know-It-All asked.

And what kind of a name was Tuesday?

Not the name of a guy, as it turned out, which we only realized when we found ourselves in front of St. Hedwig's Home for Foundling Girls.

"Foundling *Girls*?" I said. "How are we gonna be the Secret Society of He-Man Naughty Listers if the Cruel is a girl?"

"We already decided we're *not* calling ourselves that," the Brat said, getting out of the car.

The orphanage had a large stone courtyard that was walled in by a tall metal fence. It looked like a prison yard.

There were girls hanging around inside, including a really young one who was lost in some kind of imaginary game, talking to herself and hopping around on one leg.

She was playing right near the fence, so we went up to her and asked if she knew Tuesday Commons.

Whatever fantasy land she was playing in disappeared, and a look of fear came over her face. She nodded yes.

"She's not so nice, huh?" I said.

The little girl shook her head no.

"How m-m-m-mean *is* she?" the Know-It-All asked.

"So mean that her own parents gave her away when she was only six weeks old!" she whispered.

The girl told us that the Cruel was left on a *Tuesday* in the *Commons*—hence her orphan name—and that her parents pinned a note to her basket that read:

BEWARE WHOEVER TAKES THIS BABY
FOR SHE IS THE MEANEST BABY
IN THE WHOLE WORLD.
GOOD LUCK!!!
YOU'LL <u>NEED</u> IT.

Once the little girl started talking about the Cruel, it was hard to get her to stop.

The favorite part of any day for the Cruel was getting another girl to cry, she said, and an even better day was getting another girl in trouble for something she herself had done. But her very favorite thing was blackmailing the other girls into doing her chores by threatening to make up stories about them and tattling to Sister Mary Magdalen.

"And the younger and sweeter a girl is, the more she enjoys torturing them," the girl said. "I'm her favorite target!"

The most galling thing, however, was that the Cruel got away with everything. This was because she was Sister Mary Magdalen's favorite. (Sister Mary Magdalen being, like most people who ran orphanages, extremely cruel herself.)

The Brat asked the girl if the Cruel got coal in her stocking on Christmas.

"Yes!" she said, and smiled, remembering. "Oh, that was the best! The look on her face when she found that sparkly lump of coal. . . ."

Maybe the Naughty List wasn't such a bad idea after all.

The Brat asked which one the Cruel was, and the little girl's face turned fearful again as she pointed across the yard. The girl she was pointing to was tall and beautiful and had two long braids of white-blonde hair that made her look like some kind of Viking warrior princess.

"How can anyone that p-p-pretty be on the Naughty List?" the Know-It-All said.

"She ain't that pretty," I said.

"You *are* the biggest liar in the world," the Brat said.

"Well, I still don't want her in the club," I said.

"She's *definitely* in the club," the Brat said.

But which one of us had the guts to go up and talk to her? None of us, it turned out, so we shot rounds of odds and evens to see who would give her the invite.

I lost.

It seemed like it took forever for the three of us to walk around the perimeter of the fence to the other side of the courtyard. When we got near the Cruel, the Brat pushed me forward.

I went *Psst!* louder and louder until I finally got her attention.

She looked completely disgusted to see me. She actually snarled.

"What do *you* want?" she said.

As I gave her the spiel, the Cruel gave me a stare so withering—so full of loathing—that I wanted to vanish inside my coat. Or maybe even my soul.

I didn't stop feeling like I wanted to die until I handed her the invite.

She opened it.

"He-Men? Is that supposed to be the three of you?" the Cruel said with an arched eyebrow. "And what am I supposed to be—a She-Woman?"

"We're not keeping the n-n-n-n-name!" the Know-It-All said, piping up

"Yeah, it was *his* dumb idea!" the Brat said, pointing at me.

"Why on earth would I come to this *whatever* you call it?" the Cruel said, holding up the invite like it was someone else's snotty handkerchief.

"Well, it's g-g-going to be very informative," the Know-It-All said. "And we'll be discussing a p-p-p-p-petition, and—"

"**Revenge**," the Brat said, cutting off the Know-It-All. "That's why. We're going to get back at Santa for blacklisting us in favor of all the simpering nice kids of the world."

The Cruel's lips formed into an icy Viking smirk. She couldn't help herself.

She folded the invite and slipped it into her coat.

Then she swept us away with the back of her hand.

We were dismissed.

6. THREE MORE MEMBERS

There were four more kids on the list. One of them—the Cheater—wasn't home, but the other three all took the invites. Even if we wished one of them hadn't.

And that one was most definitely:

Maxwell Cooper, 12, VAINGLORIOUS

When we got to his house, his big sister answered the door and took us upstairs to the bedroom hallway.

Standing at the end of it, beside a grandfather clock, was the Vainglorious, making faces into a mirror.

If he had been making funny faces, it wouldn't have been so bad. But he was making serious faces. And angry faces. And then—*yuck*—kissy faces.

"He thinks he's gonna be a movie star," his sister said, rolling her eyes. "Like Rudolph Valentino or somebody."

The amazing thing was that he didn't stop looking at himself to say hello to us, and not when we handed him the invite, either.

"I'm trying to find my best angle," he said, sucking his cheeks in.

On top of being full of himself, the Vainglorious wasn't very bright. Nothing we said seemed the least bit surprising to him. As if random people came to his house every day saying they had found Santa's Naughty List and he was on it.

He only perked up when I told him why he was on the list.

"Because I'm glorious?"

"No. Not 'glorious,' *vain*glorious," I said.

"But there, you said it again," he said, raising a finger. "Vain*glorious*!"

"Which doesn't mean glorious," I said. "It means you like looking at yourself in the mirror too much."

"Actually," the Know-It-All said, "it originally meant 'worthless glory,' but its present definition is 'vain, excessively boastful, and possessing too much pride.'"

The Vainglorious ignored us and arched his eyebrows dramatically, his face practically touching the mirror.

I tried to take the invite back, but the Vainglorious pulled it away.

"I'm sure I will have something better to do that day," he said. "But I'd hate for your meeting to be ruined by not having the Glorious there."

"No, that's O.K.," the Know-It-All said. "You don't have to come."

"Really," the Brat said. "Don't."

"Well, I wouldn't miss it for the world," the Vainglorious said, shoving the invite in his back pocket. "The Glorious will be there!"

The last two kids *had* to be better than him, and they were. Both of them lived in the Hill District, the African American part of town. We first went looking for:

John Colson, 11, RUDE

The Rude wasn't at the boardinghouse where he lived, but the guy at the front desk told us we could find him at either the racetrack or a boxing gym called Punchin' Judy's. He had jobs at both places.

It was at Punchin' Judy's where we found him. We didn't even have to go inside, because the Rude was walking out when we arrived, carrying a pair of buckets.

"Are you John Colson?" the Brat said.

He looked the Brat up and down—mostly up, because the Rude was so short—and then the Know-It-All and me, too.

"Who wants to know?" he said, and let out a loud, open-mouthed burp. He took one of the pails—which were spit buckets—and tossed its contents onto a mound of iced-over snow, adding to an iceberg of snot, spit, and blood. The new goop oozed down until it froze, too.

It was pretty much the grossest thing I had ever seen.

"We've g-g-g-got an invite for you."

The Rude tossed out the other spit bucket and took the invite from the Know-It-All. He read it quickly and put it back in the envelope.

"Count me in," he said.

"Uh, don't you want to know more about it?" I said.

"Well, if it's a *secret* society and you're having a *secret* meeting, I figure we're not supposed to talk about it right here," he said, motioning to the people hanging out in front of the gym. "And I've got a pretty good idea of why I'm invited."

He then let out another open-mouthed burp and told us to go away.

"Before someone thinks I'm *friends* with you three or sump'm'."

Back in the car, we drove to the other side of the Hill

District—the nice side. Because it was such a well-kept part of town, the graffiti we saw on the side of a building stood out all the more. It read:

I HATE SANTA!

For graffiti, the handwriting was remarkably neat.

"Now that's *my* kind of graffiti!" the Brat said, somehow not also noting that it was remarkably coincidental. (Of course, the Know-It-All and I didn't notice it either. But still.)

The red-painted declaration was on the side of Choice's Restaurant, which was across from Choice's Grocery, which was next to Choice's Laundry.

"Choice!" the Know-It-All said. "That's the name of the last kid we're looking for!"

Mimi Choice, 12, V—

As for what the *V* stood for, we had no idea. Her naughty crime was singed off the list. And for all we knew, that *V* was half a *W*, or the middle part of an *M*.

She lived in a fancy house—not a castle like the Brat did, but a heck of a lot nicer one than any other home I had ever visited. As we walked down the path to the front door, we could hear the faint sound of a piano.

The door was answered by the V's mom.

I told her we were there on account of our church group having a Help the Orphans food drive. "We thought Mimi might be interested in volunteering."

"Oh, I'm sure Mimi would love that!" her mom said. "She's always trying to help those less fortunate. Why, do you know that she's been volunteering at the hospital? Just last week she made her first cast! It was for a poor boy who broke his arm playing football."

As we walked down the hall, the music got louder, and then stopped when we entered the parlor. The V got up from the piano as her mom introduced us. That done, she left, and the V put on a pair of glasses, like she didn't want her mom to see she was wearing them.

Now, why would someone have to hide wearing glasses from their *mother*?

But the V was different in lots of ways. She didn't act like the other kids when the Know-It-All told her why we were really there. The others all got angry at being on the Naughty List or pretended not to care.

Mimi burst into tears.

"Yes, YES, it's true!" she sobbed. "I'm not nice enough! In April, I lied about feeling sick so I wouldn't have to go to choir practice. And not only that! On the Fourth of July, I stayed up past my bedtime *on purpose* so I could watch the fireworks. And sometimes I don't even listen in school!"

The three of us looked at each other.

"M-m-maybe Santa made a mistake," the Know-It-

All said. "If that's all you did, then every kid in the world would be on the N-N-N-Naughty List."

"Yeah," I said. "The rest of us are *really* bad. Like, all the time!"

But that didn't mean she couldn't come to our meeting, so I handed her the invite. (The HE-MAN was now scribbled out, so it just read THE SECRET SOCIETY OF ~~HE-MAN~~ NAUGHTY LISTERS.)

"It's a very nice-looking invitation," she said, and blew her nose. She then showed us to the door and waved goodbye.

Of course, the V knew exactly why she was on the Naughty List. And it had nothing to do with pretending to be sick or not listening in school.

◆ ◆ ◆

On the drive home, I counted up all of our successfully invited Naughty Listers.

"There are the three of us," I said, "plus the Lazy, Cruel, Vainglorious, Rude, and Goody-Two-Shoes back there. That's nine. So, how about this: we call ourselves the **Naughty Nine!**"

"You counted wrong," the Know-It-All said. "That's only eight."

I counted again, this time on my fingers. The Know-It-All was right, dang it. I always did stink at math.

"Well, it's *still* a great name."

"No it's not," the Brat said. "I don't want to be called the *Naughty* anything."

"Well, how about the *Notorious* Nine?" I said.

The Brat shook his head.

"The *Nefarious* Nine?"

Still no.

"The *Nitwit* Nine?"

"Can't you do any better?" the Brat said. "These names are no good at all!"

"That's **it**!" I said, snapping my fingers. "*No good! That's us!* THE NO-GOOD NINE!"

"But we're *not* nine!" the Know-It-All said. "We're *eight*!"

The Brat pointed out that we'd probably be even fewer than that. "There's no way the Lazy will make it out of bed. And if not paying attention in class is her worst crime, Goody-Two-Shoes is not going to want to run away from home with a bunch of No-Good-*whatever*-we-are and break into Santa's workshop."

"I don't think it's very nice the way you two are calling her Goody-Two-Shoes," the Know-It-All spoke up from the back seat. "Her name is M-M-Mimi."

"*Oooooh!*" I said. "The Know-It-All's got a crush!"

"Do not!"

"You do!" the Brat said.

"Do n-n-n-not!"

Teasing the Know-It-All was the most fun we'd had all day. But if we had been making less fun of him and paying more attention, we might have noticed that we were being followed.

As for who was following us, well, I should've known.

It was my archenemy.

Yes, that's right. I was twelve years old and I had an archenemy.

And I'm not lying.*

*He's really not. —The Editor

EPISODE TWO:
ESCAPE FROM PITTSBURGH

7. THE FIRST OFFICIAL MEETING OF THE NO-GOOD NINE COMES TO ORDER

The Brat was wrong about Goody-Two-Shoes. She did show up, and right on time.

She wasn't the first one, though. The Rude was at the factory even before the Brat, the Know-It-All, and I pulled up in the Doozy.

If the Rude hadn't said much at the boxing gym, it wasn't because he didn't like to talk. In fact, he hardly ever stopped. He only paused when Goody-Two-Shoes arrived. And then when the next Naughty Lister came.

The next one being—unfortunately—the Vainglorious.

"The meeting can start!" he said. "The Glorious is here!"

Just as he and the other two were getting acquainted, the door opened again. It let in a frigid blast of cold air, as well as the Cruel.

She didn't so much as wave to us, let alone come over to talk to us. And none of us were going to go talk to *her*.

Well, none of us except the Vainglorious.

"Finally, another attractive person!" he said. "I was afraid I had joined some sort of ugly club."

The Cruel gave him a withering stare. The kind that would turn your toes to icicles.

I was starting to like her.

Goody-Two-Shoes, however, was not. In fact, she didn't seem to approve of any of the other recruits. Not the Vainglorious (for obvious reasons) and not the Rude either. Every time the Rude burped or picked his nose—both of which he did a *lot*—it seemed to cause her physical pain. She began looking around the factory like she was trying to find an escape route.

The factory, by the way, was aces. (Yet another way of saying cool.) It was owned by the Brat's family and it was where they used to make grenades and bombs back in the Great War. Since there wasn't much need for that kind of stuff anymore, it was now empty. Or, rather, it had just become the world's biggest secret clubhouse.

"It's time to start the meeting," the Brat said.

I said we couldn't—"Not everyone is here yet!"—but the Brat said he wasn't waiting for the Lazy to show up. He banged a gavel and called the meeting to order.

"Why do *you* get to call the meeting to order?" I said.

"Because *I* am paying for everyone, *I* own the building, and *I* have the gavel," the Brat said, holding up the wooden mallet.

I had to admit—those were good reasons. Where'd he get the gavel from, anyway?

As the Brat finished welcoming everyone, someone else did walk in.

But it wasn't the Lazy.

No, it was someone no one could believe. At least, not any of the three of us who had already met him.

It was the Hooligan!

Of the Mug Uglies.

The kid who had tried to kill us!

(Or at least hurt us real bad.)

"What are *you* doing here?" the Brat said.

The Hooligan looked sheepish. He couldn't pretend like he had happened into this abandoned factory by accident—like he didn't *want* to be at our meeting.

"I said, what are *you* doing here?" the Brat repeated.

The Hooligan shrugged.

"I wanna get back at Santa," he said. "He ain't never given me a present. Not ever! All the other Mug Uglies have gotten a present at least once. Even my big brother Jimmy. And he's on Death Row!"

All at once, the rest of the Naughty Listers started yelling over each other.

The Rude—"Yeah! I know way worse kids than me that *always* get presents!"

The Cruel—"I've *never* gotten a present either!"

The Vainglorious—"How could *I* not get a present?"

The Brat—"Santa must pay for stiffing us!"

The Hooligan—"Yeah!"

"But what if we *do* all deserve it?"

Everyone stopped shouting and stared at Goody-Two-Shoes.

"Who let *her* in?" the Cruel said.

"Yeah! She doesn't belong!" the Rude said. "She's rich! Her parents can buy her whatever present she wants."

"She does too belong!" the Know-It-All said. He held up the charred paper. "Anyone who's on this list b-b-b-belongs. The question we have to ask is whether or not this *list* should exist!"

This was the moment the Know-It-All had been waiting for ever since he had come up with his plan. He would convince us all, and together we would change the world!

"There m-m-must be a reason why this list fell into our hands," he continued. "Yes, we all want presents. Yes, we are all mad at Santa. But what will we *d-d-do* about it?"

The Hooligan and the Rude both shrugged.

"We will present Santa with a list of our own!" the Know-It-All said, answering his question. He was on such a roll, he had even stopped stuttering. "A list of de-mands! A list of rights for the children of the world on the day that was *made* for the children of the world—Christmas! We will make Santa see the error of his ways and stop dividing children into who is Naughty and who is Nice. Together, we will make Christmas a holiday for ALL!"

The Know-It-All was finished. He looked triumphant. The speech came out just like he had been practicing it.

"Uh, that sounds pretty good and all," the Rude said. "But I just wanna go play with the toys of the nice kids of the world."

"Me too!" the Hooligan said.

"And I still want to punch that fat old elf in the stom-ach!" the Brat said.

"I'm with bow tie boy," the Cruel said.

"I wanna play with the toys *and* punch him in the stomach," the Hooligan said.

"Yeah!" the Rude said.

"But if we do that, we'll be just as bad—as *naughty*—as Santa thinks!" Goody-Two-Shoes said. "The Know-It-All is right!"

"But we *are* bad. And naughty!" the Rude said. "Most of us, anyway."

Only the Vainglorious wasn't saying anything. He had found a reflection of himself in the window and was doing that arched eyebrow thing again. I doubt he had any clue what we were even talking about.

But everyone else had an opinion, and the meeting spiraled into total chaos. This was what we should have expected, getting a bunch of Naughty Listers together. It was up to me to get things back on track.

Plus, I really wanted to try that gavel.

BANG! BANG! BANG!

It got everyone's attention.

"Look," I said, waving the gavel in the air. "Why do we have to do just one thing or the other? Present a petition *or* play with toys? Make Christmas fair *or* punch Santa in the stomach? If the No-Good Nine is about anything—"

"But there are only eight—"

"If we're about *any*thing," I repeated, cutting Goody-Two-Shoes off, "we should be about doing whatever the heck we want!"

I turned to the Know-It-All. "You do want to play with the toys of the nice kids of the world, right?"

"Well, yeah . . ."

"So we're agreed!" I said.

There was a cheer and applause, and I had to bang the gavel again. I loved banging the gavel.

"The first motion of the No-Good Nine—"

"But there are only—"

"Of the No-Good Nine is decided," I said. "We will go to Santa's factory, where we will play with the toys of all the nice children of the world and present him with a petition. *Then* we'll slug him!"

"DOWN WITH SANTA!"

"TOYS! TOYS! TOYS!"

Now, you might be asking yourself, Why do all these kids care so much about toys?

The answer is that it wasn't really about the toys.

Has there ever been a party you didn't get invited to and even though the person wasn't your friend, you still wished that you *had* been?

Or did you ever ask for a present that you never got and you still wanted it even though it wasn't the kind of thing you liked anymore?

And has anyone ever been wrong about you and you just couldn't get over it?

Well, *those* were the kinds of reasons why we wanted to break into Santa's factory and play with the toys of the nice kids of the world.

(Those, plus I always wanted my own baseball bat.)

But do you know who didn't care one bit about why we were going to Santa's?

The guy outside. The one eavesdropping on our meeting.

My archenemy!

8. MY ARCHENEMY

I count eight children inside.

They are plotting to take over Santa's workshop and steal all the toys therein.

They are also plotting to do physical harm to Santa himself.

I do not yet understand how they plan to get there.

From where I hide outside the window, I cannot hear everything, but I hear enough.

These children must be stopped!

For the purposes of telling this story, it is a lucky break that my archenemy wrote everything down in his journal. And when I say everything, I mean *everything*. He even wrote down what was happening *while* it was happening.

It is also fortunate that I was able to get my hands on his journals. Not that I myself could read them. That's because his writing looked like this:

Эти дети должны быть остановлены!

My archenemy, you see, was Russian. And not just any Russian, but a former secret agent of the tsar, whose secret agents were pretty much the most terrifying secret agents in the whole entire world.

Or at least they were until the revolution. That's when the tsar got killed, and all his agents had to flee Russia or get killed themselves, which is how my particular nemesis—Ivan Ivanovich—wound up in Pittsburgh.

His having been a top-flight spy back in his own country didn't mean much in America, unfortunately for the both of us. As much as the guy dearly wanted to be a secret agent again, or a military officer, or at the very least a cop, the only job he could get in the U.S. of A. was as a truant officer.

Now, you probably go to school without being hounded by an officer of the law, but it wasn't like that in 1931. Back then, truant officers were a special kind of police force whose job was to hunt down children who were skipping school.

It was my particular misfortune that not only had my school hired an obsessive Russian secret agent to be their truant officer, but he considered any kid who skipped school once in a while to be a hardened criminal.

And I skipped school a *lot*.

Normally, I stayed on the lookout for the Truant Officer, but that week I had let my guard down. For good reason. We were on Christmas vacation!

I should've known that that wasn't enough reason for my archenemy to stay home.

I would find out later what had happened: The Truant Officer had been driving his beat-up black jalopy down the street when he saw me and the Know-It-All walking to the Brat's. He figured this was suspicious behavior and followed us, and kept following us, even the next day when we went into Pittsburgh to recruit the other kids. And he hadn't stopped spying on us yet.

This crazy truant officer believed he had stumbled onto some kind of nefarious criminal conspiracy of bad-intentioned kids.

Which I guess he kind of had.

9. THE FIRST OFFICIAL MEETING OF THE NO-GOOD NINE CONTINUES

And now for the *rest* of the meeting.

First, the Know-It-All laid out his plan. It was so boring, it was like being in school, so I didn't pay any attention. Heck, I could hardly stay awake.

Those who *were* able to listen heard about the magical lighthouse, and how once we got there, we'd use its signal as a kind of enormous telegraph, transmitting a flashing message in Morse code. This message would call a giant narwhal—whatever *that* was—to come fetch us. Apparently the narwhal came hauling a barge behind it like some kind of oversize mule of the sea.

As for how the Know-It-All knew this, he said he'd read about it in a magazine.

"If it's so easy to get to Toyland," the Cruel said, "then why isn't everyone doing it?"

The Know-It-All perked up at the question. (I think he was just happy someone was still listening.)

"That's an excellent point!" he said. "The writer of the article swore never to reveal the w-w-whereabouts of the lighthouse. He did, however, mention that the lighthouse is in Labrador and—"

"Wait, what does a dog have to do with this?" the Hooligan said.

"Not a dog—there's a *place* called Labrador."

"My family has a Labrador!" the Vainglorious said. "His name is Rex."

"No no no," the Know-It-All said. "I'm not talking about a dog, I'm talking about a p-p-part of Newfound-land!"

There were lots of lighthouses in Labrador, but the Know-It-All had figured out which one it was because of a photo in the article.

"It shows the lighthouse keeper posing with a Chance Bros 55 mm I.O.V. Lamp."

"So?" the Rude said.

"So, there is only one l-l-lighthouse in all of Labrador that uses the Chance 55 mm, at least according to the documents I was able to find," the Know-It-All said, like it was the most exciting thing in the world. "And that lighthouse is in Black Tickle, located at a latitude and longitude of 53.47° north and 55.79° west."

"You're making my brain hurt," the Hooligan said.

My feelings exactly.

"Look, all you dopes need to know is that the Know-It-All has figured out where this magic lighthouse is," the Brat said, "and that from there, we can get to Santa's workshop."

Next the Know-It-All gave us our itinerary—the trains and boats we were going to take—with the rail portion of the journey taking us from Pittsburgh to Quebec City.

"We'll be l-l-leaving on the 5:59 p.m. train from Union Station on New Year's Eve, which is to say this Thursday," he said. "We will meet thirty minutes ahead of time—5:29 p.m.—at the mailbox just inside the south entrance to the station."

"But how are we supposed to pay for all these trains and boats?" the Hooligan asked.

"I already bought the tickets," the Brat said, and gave me the nod to start handing them out. "And as I paid for them, I expect you all to follow my orders."

"Hey, that ain't fair!" the Hooligan said.

"If anyone would like to pay for their own ticket, I'd be happy to sell them one. They cost fifteen dollars and thirty-six cents." Which, in 1931, was a small fortune. Or a big one, if you were me. "Any takers?"

As the Brat waited for somebody to speak up, the Cruel shot him a look so hateful, anyone else would have rephrased what they had just said.

Not the Brat.

"I didn't think so!" he said, and banged the gavel.

"I do have a question," Goody-Two-Shoes said, raising her hand. "Won't we be missing an awful lot of school?"

"To hell with school!" the Rude said, and everyone cheered.

To [heck] with school! one of them says, my nemesis wrote in his journal, crouched down in his hiding spot. *And the other kids cheer!*

The last thing the Know-It-All told us was that we weren't allowed to tell anyone what we were doing. Not a brother or a sister, or even a best friend.

"And definitely not your parents!"

"But won't they be worried about us?" Goody-Two-Shoes said.

The Know-It-All said that each of us should write letters to our loved ones, explaining that we were on a "mission" but without revealing what we were doing or where we were going. We would drop our letters in the mailbox at the train station. "By the time the letters get to our homes, we'll be long gone," he said.

With all the boring stuff out of the way, it was finally *my* turn to talk. I had important secret society matters to address.

"Like names!"

"Good," the Cruel said. "Because the No-Good Nine is the worst name ever. Especially since there are only eight of us."

"I'm talking about *our* names," I said. "Because this is a secret society, we can't use our real names. From now on, we only refer to each other by our No-Good Names. So I am no longer Looie, but the Liar. And you are the Cruel."

She actually smiled. "Fine by me."

"And everyone must call me Glorious!"

"*Vain*glorious, you moron," the Brat said. "How many times do we have to tell you?"

I next told everyone the secret password—*It's me, stupid!*—and showed them the secret sign, which I had been working on for two days. You made it by crossing your arms over your chest and flashing five fingers on your right hand and four on your left.

"Just don't use your left thumb," I said, demonstrating. "It's the Sign of the Nine! Pretty jake, right?"

"That is the most idiotic, childish thing I have ever seen in my life," the Cruel said.

"And there's an oath!" I said, almost forgetting. "If you're with us, flash the sign and say, *One for nine, and nine for one!*"

"That doesn't make any sense," the Know-It-All said. "On so many levels."

While that might have been true, it sounded swell and that was all that mattered.

"Now, who's with us?" I said, and flashed the sign.

I waited for everyone to flash it back. The Cruel shook her head no like she wouldn't do it. But she did.

"One for nine, and nine for one!"

10. WHAT HAPPENED ON THE WAY HOME

The children are leaving!

I rush to my car and duck down in the driver's seat so I won't be seen.

I sit hiding, but I have learned much of their plan.

The children will be meeting at Union Station in Pittsburgh on 31 December.

Time: Unknown.

Destination: Unknown.

I will continue following them in hopes of learning more details.

When we walked out, I noticed the beat-up old black jalopy parked across the street, but I didn't recognize it. It just looked abandoned and—like I said—I assumed my archenemy was on vacation.

Saying goodbye to the other Ninesters was kind of awkward. Goody-Two-Shoes left first, and then the Rude and the Hooligan followed her, all of them going in the same direction. Goody-Two-Shoes looked less than thrilled about the company, but was too polite to say anything.

The Know-It-All and I started walking to the Doozy, and that's when the Brat offered to give the Cruel a ride home.

I understood why he did it—I mean, I *was* lying when I said she wasn't that beautiful. But I was amazed he had the guts.

It didn't work out so well for him.

"You have a car! Fantastic!" the Vainglorious said. "I'll come too!"

"Who asked *you* to come?" the Brat said. The Vainglorious, however, was already in the back seat, primping in the rearview mirror.

I went to get in the front seat, but the Brat blocked me. "What are you, some sort of barbarian?" he said. "The girl gets the front seat!"

If the Brat thought this chivalry act was going to score points with the Cruel, he had another think coming.

"I hope you don't think I'm impressed by this car," she said as we bumped along in the Doozy. "Or the fact that you can drive it—badly. Because that would be sad and pathetic."

"HAH! She sure crusted *you*!" the Vainglorious yelled from the back seat.

The Brat's face started going that color again.

We dropped off the Vainglorious first, then the Cruel, and the three of us made the long drive back to Sewickley. The Brat stopped the car about a mile outside of town.

"Get out," he said.

"Hey, what's the big idea?" I said. "Aren't you driving us home, too?"

"You guys live that way," he said, pointing to the right. "And I live that way," he said, pointing left. "I have to get home before my father realizes the car is gone."

"So you can't take five minutes to take us into town?"

"What are you complaining about?" the Brat said as the Know-It-All and I got out. "It's downhill! Hah!"

"Jerk!" I yelled as he drove off.

The worst part of the walk was how the Know-It-All wouldn't stop yammering about Morse code and lighthouse reflectors. It seemed like we had walked a hundred miles by the time we got to his house.

Instead of heading home myself, I ambled over to Beaver Street. I had a nickel burning a hole in my pocket, and there was some rock candy at the confectionary with my name on it.

As I crossed Broad Street, I almost got hit by a beat-up jalopy.

Which was the *same* beat-up jalopy I had seen at the meeting place! I looked at it more closely now. It was a black Tin Lizzie with a missing rumble seat. And I knew *exactly* who had one of those!

I kept on strolling down the sidewalk. Out of the corner of my eye, I watched the jalopy slowly following me. Then I passed a parked delivery truck which blocked the street-side view, and I quick ducked into Slam's Barber Shop.

"Hey, Looie!" the barber said. "How's that momma a yers?"

"Pretty good, Slam!" I said, walking through his storeroom and out into the alley. I looped back around and up the street, right to where the jalopy was still waiting.

Ducking low, I snuck up alongside the car, opened the passenger door, and popped into the front seat.

"*Blin!*" the Truant Officer shouted as he just about leapt out of his skin.

I chuckled.

"Why so jumpy?" I said. "And what does *blin* mean?"

"It means you are a *negodnik* American child!"

The Truant Officer wasn't what you would imagine a

Russian secret agent to look like. There was no big bushy beard or fur hat or anything. Instead, the guy was rail thin with blond hair and blue eyes. Really *blue* eyes. Like the sky.

And while his car might have been a mess, the Truant Officer himself was neat as a pin. His shirt was so ironed and starched, it looked more like armor than fabric, and his dumb *Sewickley Constable of Attendance* badge was polished to a shine so bright, you'd have thought it was made of real silver.

I asked him what he was following me for. "Don't you know there's no school at Christmas in this country?"

The Truant Officer stretched his lips in what must've been his version of a smile, the first I'd ever seen from him.

I didn't like it.

"Oh, I know all about your Christmas. And your Christmas *plans*," he said. "Maybe if you tell me now, the police will go easy on you!"

"What are you talking about?" I said, squinting.

"I am onto you!" He wagged a finger at me. "You and your *negodnik* friends!"

"Onto what?"

"Your plot!"

I saw the journal on the seat beside him. There was a pen stuck in the middle of it. I grabbed it and opened it.

"You cannot do that!" he yelled, trying to grab it back from me. "That is official Constable of Attendance business!"

This might have been a triumphant moment. Might have been, except—again—it was all written in Russian. But I couldn't let that stop me.

"Ah-ha! This is *very* interesting!" I said, flipping through the pages and bluffing. "So you've been following me around all week, have you? So you know about our secret club, do you?"

"Yes, I do!" he said, still trying and failing to snatch the notebook away. "And I know you are trying to destroy Christmas!"

"Destroy Christmas?" I said. "You've got it all wrong, T.O.!" He hated it when I called him by the initials. "It's a backgammon club!"

He narrowed his eyes to slits. "And you need to take a train to play backgammon? Or don't you think I know about your little plan to meet at Union Station?"

Now he smiled for real.

This was the *uh-oh* moment. What if he knew *all* our plans? But even if he did, what could he do to us? His job was just to make sure we got to school, and we'd be long gone way before we missed any class.

Still, I wasn't going to tell him the truth or anything crazy like that.

"Union Station?" I said. "That's just our meeting

place. Where else can we set up board games and no one is going to bother us?"

"We shall see about this," the Truant Officer said, and scowled as menacingly as he was able. "I always catch my man! Even when they are children."

"Well, I'm sure if anyone can break up a gang of twelve-year-old backgammon players, it's you," I said. "Now, how about you drive me to the confectionary?"

A dumbfounded look broke over his face.

"Why would I want to help *you*?"

"Well, if you're trying to follow me, then *I* am the one helping *you*," I said. "If I'm sitting right next to you in the car, I can't give you the slip!"

Grumbling, my archenemy turned the key and popped the stick into gear.

When we got to the candy store, I thanked him for the ride. He drove off without saying anything.

And without realizing I still had his journal.

11. HOW TO RUN AWAY FROM HOME

Reading in your lovely twenty-first-century library or on your comfortable twenty-first-century couch or in your own twenty-first-century bed in your own twenty-first-century room, you might be wondering what all of us Naughty Listers were thinking. After all, why would we be so quick to run away from home?

Well, I can only tell you what *I* was thinking. And that was:

Why hadn't I run away sooner?

My life was horrible. My "house" wasn't even a house. It was an apartment over a laundry. And it wasn't *our* apartment. After my dad lost his construction job, we moved in with our aunt and uncle and their five kids, which sounds like a lot of children until you realize that I had seven brothers and sisters. Plus there were three grandparents and some guy named Nunzio, who I'm not even sure was related to us. That's *twenty-one* people. And my mother was pregnant again. And so was my older sister. And my grandmother!

O.K., not my grandmother.

Anyway, the mere thought of not having to fight over every last scrap of food at dinner made the thought of leaving home sound positively delightful. (That, plus I had a book report due the first day back at school, and I hate reading anything that isn't the comics.)

You also have to understand that in 1931, it wasn't so weird to run away from home. Heck, parents half the time didn't mind—one less kid to support. Plus, kids our age could get jobs and even rent a bed in a flophouse, like the Rude did. For him, running away was easy.

The Hooligan didn't exactly live in the lap of luxury,

either, and the Cruel's orphanage was more like a prison than a home, so I wasn't surprised those two wanted to come along.

But why kids like Goody-Two-Shoes or the Brat wanted to run away, I had no idea. Heck, I'd run away to go *live* at their houses. The Vainglorious and the Know-It-All had it pretty fat from where I was sitting, too.

Which is all a way of saying it was no big deal for me to slurp up the two sips of soup that was my dinner, leave without saying goodbye to anybody, and walk three blocks to the Sewickley train station.

The Know-It-All was there waiting for me, holding a big suitcase. "Where's yours?" he asked as we walked to the Pittsburgh-bound platform.

I didn't have one. After all, I only owned one jacket and one pair of shoes, and why bother bringing extra shirts or pants? So I just took what I was wearing.

(I did have an extra pair of underwear in my pocket. I wasn't a complete animal.)

The Know-It-All, on the other hand, had spent three days packing. Besides a handkerchief and a change of clothes and a blanket, he took all the stuff we needed to make it to Santa's, like a compass and a sextant (whatever the heck *that* was). He'd also spent two days in the library copying loads of information into notebooks—not only the full text of the Santa article, but a list of Morse code symbols, the train and boat schedules, travel guides to Canada, and maps. He loved copying maps.

"And I keep worrying about what I'm forgetting!" he said as we got on the train and found seats.

Then he took out his briefcase. What twelve-year-old has a briefcase? It was even weirder than the Brat's tie.

Anyway, he unsnapped it and drew out a stack of letters. There were two each addressed to his mother, father, little sister, and grandmother.

Why *two*?

"In case one gets l-l-lost in the mail," he said. "Where are yours?"

I hadn't written any. I seriously doubted anyone in my family would even notice I was gone. Besides, writing a letter was like homework, and running away from home should *not* have homework.

"I had a feeling this would be the case," the Know-It-All said, tut-tutting me like one of my teachers. He reached back into his briefcase and brought out a stamped envelope that had *The Curidi Family* and my address written across the front of it. He handed me a sheet of paper and a pen.

"Oh, fine!" I said, taking the pen.

It took me the rest of the train ride to write the letter. It read:

Deer Familee,

*As you may or may not have notissed, I have
not bin arownd for sume time now. I have run
away frum home.*

Yer welcume.

Luve, Looie

*PS If I nevver come back, do NOT givve my
baseball cards to Littel Tony. Thancks.*

As I put the letter in the envelope and licked the back,
the conductor came walking into our train car.

"Next stop, Pittsburgh!" he hollered. "Union Station!"

I felt a jolt of excitement. It was happening! We were
really doing this!

The Know-It-All, however, didn't look excited. He sat
there clutching his suitcase, looking out the window, not
getting up.

I asked what was wrong

"Is this not a g-g-good idea?" he asked.

He had that same about-to-barf look he'd had in the
Doozy.

"Is *what* not a good idea?" I said.

"R-r-r-running away from home," he said. "Going to
C-C-Canada to try and find this lighthouse. Going to *S-
S-S-Santa's.*"

"What are you asking *me* for?" I said. "It's YOUR idea!"

"But what if something g-g-g-goes wrong?"

This should have been the moment *I* started to worry. And yet, somehow, I still thought it was going to all work out.

Did I mention that I never did have very good judgment?

12. SHOWDOWN AT UNION STATION

As we walked through the cavernous train station, I looked around for the Truant Officer. No sign of him—thank goodness!

Goody-Two-Shoes was at the meeting spot already, which put a smile on the Know-It-All's face. The two of them compared how many letters they had written and what they had packed. (Goody-Two-Shoes's luggage contained sewing equipment, which the Know-It-All thought was splendid.)

Next came the Brat, who had a monogrammed steamer trunk that was twice the size of the Know-It-All's and Goody-Two-Shoes's suitcases put together. Of course, he had that yellow-uniformed servant of his to carry it for him.

Not that the servant knew about our plan. The Brat's parents had sent him to the train station because he was supposed to be heading back to boarding school in New Hampshire. (Which, it winds up, was *his* idea of prison, and the real reason he was running away.)

The servant would naturally be carrying the trunk for him, but the Brat had a better idea.

"Why don't we let one of these poor boys who hang around the station looking for tips take it for me?" he said. "Like that really filthy one over there!"

He pointed at me.

At first, I wanted to pop him right in his grinning mug. But I didn't.

"Oh, yessir, sir!" I said, saluting him. "Thank you so much for the opportunity, sir! And I'll take that tip right up front, please, sir. Fifty cents, please, sir!"

Which—believe it or not—was a lot of money.

"Fifty cents! That's robbery!" the Brat said. "An outrage!"

The servant stepped up and gave me the money out of his own pocket.

"It's well worth it, if it means spending one less minute with him," the servant said, jerking his head back toward the Brat. "Have fun."

I looked at the shiny quarters. Money!

"Well?" the Brat said, holding a hand out to the trunk and looking at me.

"Ah, move it yourself!" I said.

Just then, the Hooligan and the Rude arrived. Together.

Apparently, they had become fast friends since they walked home together after the meeting. Go figure.

The Rude had packed, but it couldn't have been much. Whatever he had was wrapped inside of a handkerchief and tied to the end of a broomstick.

"What are you, a hobo?" the Brat said. "And how about you?" He turned to the Hooligan. "Or did you bring absolutely nothing, like the Liar over here?"

"Ah, I don't need nuttin'. Not so long as I got my lucky rabbit's foot!" The Hooligan patted his chest to feel for it, and a look of panic swept over him. "My lucky rabbit's foot! I forgot it! I hafta go home and get it!"

"What? Wait!" the Rude called after him. "You'll never make it back in time! Just forget it!"

But the Hooligan was already gone.

"Don't worry," I said. "He's got half an hour. He'll make it!"

Which wasn't 100 percent a lie, because I didn't know *for sure* he wouldn't make it. I just assumed.

The Cruel came next, holding one small bag. I smiled and waved.

She did not wave back.

"Do you have a letter?" the Know-It-All asked her.

"Most *definitely*," the Cruel said, grinning. "It says what I think of every single one of those sniveling girls I have had to live with over the past thirteen years. And the nuns too! I've been waiting to send a letter like this my entire life."

"I'm sure they'll be real sorry to see you go," I said.

Everyone had at least one letter to mail except the Vainglorious, who was the last to show.

"What's this about a letter?" he said. "It's the first I'm hearing of it!"

"That's because you never listen to a single thing we say," I said.

"I listen to what *she* says," he said, and winked at the Cruel, who narrowed her nostrils and rolled her eyes.

The letters mailed, we headed over to the departure board to see which track our train would be departing from. And that was when I saw him.

My archenemy. The Truant Officer!

He was wearing what had to be the single worst disguise in the history of mankind. He had on a big bushy fake black beard and a fur hat. *Now* he looked like a Russian secret agent.

"Uh, guys," I said, stopping everyone dead in their tracks. "We might have a problem."

I gave them the whole story.

"You're just telling us this **now**?" the Brat said, going beet red in the face. "What were you thinking, you nitwit!"

"Hey, no need to get mean!" I said. "I thought I had thrown him off our trail."

"Well, I guess you didn't, did you?" the Brat said.

I explained how it wasn't like he could do anything to us. "We're not skipping school or anything," I said. "It's New Year's Eve!"

"But we *are* running away from home!" the Brat said. "We can get arrested for *that*!"

"We can?" I said.

"And thrown into juvenile d-d-d-detention," the Know-It-All added.

O.K., so maybe I *had* messed up. Still, everyone was making a big deal out of nothing. I'd been giving this Truant Officer guy the slip for years—it was not that hard! Plus he obviously didn't know which train we were taking, so all we needed to do was stay away from him. Once we had the track number, we'd slip onto the train and be gone.

"But what about the Hooligan?" the Rude said.

"He's on his own!" the Cruel said.

We hid behind a column in a place where my nemesis couldn't see us but we could keep our eye on the clock and the destination board.

"Where are we going again?" the Vainglorious said.

"Don't you pay attention to *anything*?" the Rude said. "We're going to Quebec. Canada!"

"Canada?" the Vainglorious said. "Oh yes—of course,

Canada! One of the original thirty states."

"There were *thirteen* original states," the Cruel said. "And Canada is a country."

"It's cute how much you like me," the Vainglorious said. "The way you correct me and all."

"Does he *have* to come?" she said to the Know-It-All and the Brat. They shrugged.

The numbers on the board started to flip, and our train got assigned to track 8. We had ten minutes to board.

The Rude wanted to wait for the Hooligan, but we dragged him away.

"Don't worry, he can figure it out," I said, now 99 percent lying.

We snuck around the outer edges of the terminal. The biggest problem was the Brat's trunk. I did wind up helping with it—I'm honest *that* way—but it was the size of a small house and too heavy to carry. We had to drag it, with the Rude pushing from behind. It was LOUD!

"What've you got in here?" the Rude said. "Rocks?"

"Don't be ridiculous. It's full of clothes," the Brat said. "And silver coins."

We stopped to look at him.

He shrugged. "We need *money*, remember?"

"I should be getting more than half a buck for this!" I said.

"Wait," the Rude said. "You got *paid*?"

"No," I said. "Not at all."

Even with the noise of the dragging, the Truant Officer never looked once in our direction. He just kept writing in his journal.

Train station crowded.

I stand my post, still in my impenetrable disguise.

No sign of the children anywhere.

No wonder he never managed to catch me!

When we finally finished dragging the trunk to track 8, the Brat pointed ahead and told us to put it in first class.

"You put yourself in first class and you put *us* back in third class?" the Rude said.

"Of course I did!" he said. "That's where the servants always sit."

"Well, push this the rest of the way yourself, then," the Rude said, giving the trunk a kick and walking away. "I'm gettin' on the train!"

Before he did, though, he looked around the station for the Hooligan.

Still no sign of him.

"*All aboard!*" the conductor yelled.

We all got seats, except the Rude, who stood on the

steps by the open door, searching for his pal. About a minute before the train was supposed to leave, he saw him. He wanted to yell but he couldn't.

The Hooligan was standing right next to the Truant Officer!

How could that Russian not see him? And what was the Hooligan doing just standing there?

"He can't figure out which train we're on!" the Rude said. "How are we gonna let him know and not get caught?"

If you wanted smarts, you needed the Know-It-All. If it was money, the Brat. But sneakiness? That was *my* department.

"Hey, Glorious," I said.

The Vainglorious smiled, pleased someone had finally called him *Glorious*.

"The Cruel left her bag on the platform," I said, talking as fast as I could. "Do you see that guy over there in the big beard with the furry hat? He brought it for her. Can you go run and get it?"

"Why should I be the one to do it?" he said.

"Because the train's about to leave and none of us can run as fast as you!" I said.

"Well, that is surely true. . . ."

"Please?" the Cruel said, and batted her eyes at him. "You'll be my hero!"

He smiled a dopey smile.

"You've gotta run—now! Go!" I said, slapping him on the back. The Vainglorious made a dash down the steps of the train, like he was the star of some adventure serial.

"And make sure you tell him you're with the **No-Good Nine**!" I called after him.

At the same moment, the Truant Officer finally stopped writing in his journal long enough to realize who was standing next to him.

"You!" he said to the Hooligan. "You are coming with me, you *negodnik* runaway!"

Before he could grab him, however, the Vainglorious stepped in between them.

"I'm with the **No-Good Nine**!" he said proudly.

"**Hooligan!**" we all yelled from the train. "**RUN!**"

The Hooligan saw us all hanging out the windows of the train and took off as fast as he could.

"All aboard! Last call!!"

"What are you doing?" the Vainglorious said as my archenemy handcuffed him. "Where's the Cruel's bag?"

The Truant Officer left the Vainglorious standing there and took off after the Hooligan. He was a lot faster than he looked. Even with the beard.

The train started to move *CHUG-chug CHUG-chug.*

The Hooligan made a leap for the Rude's outstretched arm—grabbed it!—and the Rude pulled him in. I slammed the door shut behind the Hooligan, right in the face of my nemesis.

"**STOP!**" the Truant Officer hollered, running alongside the train. He tapped his shiny badge against the glass. "**STOP** in the name of the tsar!" he yelled. "I mean, **STOP** in the name of the Sewickley Department of Attendance!"

We all stuck our heads out the windows as the train overtook him.

I was a little sorry to say goodbye to him.

But I was the only one.

"So long, sucker!" the Hooligan yelled.

The Cruel blew kisses to the Vainglorious. "Bye-bye, hero!!"

The Rude had his own way of saying goodbye. He jumped up on a seat, pulled his pants down, and stuck his butt out the window.

"Enjoy the full moon!"

My archenemy's face went white, while the Vainglorious looked dumber than ever. We all cheered.

Except for Goody-Two-Shoes. She just whispered to herself,

"What have I gotten myself into?"

EPISODE THREE:
THE THIEF

13. HAPPY 1932!

"So, what are all you kids doing on a train alone, eh?"

"We're the youth group of the International Geographical Explorers Club. We're collecting samples of Canadian snow to compare against American snow."

"Well, that's interesting, eh?" the lady said.

It was already the fifth story I'd made up on the ride. With each one, the Cruel shot me an ever-icier look.

She was stuck in the seat next to me. Or rather, I was stuck next to *her*.

The girl was terrifying! But all the other seats were taken.

The two pals—the Rude and the Hooligan—sat next to each other right in front of us. In the aisle across from them were the Know-It-All and Goody-Two-Shoes, who were quickly becoming just as tight a pair. It was as if being smart and nice had drawn them together like magnets. Honestly, I think it was a mistake *either* of them was on the Naughty List.

The Brat, of course, was all alone up in first class. Not that anyone would have wanted to sit next to him anyway, let alone become best pals with him. Because he was, well, a *brat*. But I still would've taken him over my present seatmate.

I was trying to think of something to say to her when the Cruel said, "Don't even think of talking to me. And don't look at me."

She tapped the armrest between us.

"You see this? This is *mine*. Pretend that there's an invisible force field that extends from here up. And if you accidentally cross it, you *die*. Got it?"

I gulped. And nodded.

"It's time! It's time!" a passenger from the seats in back began to yell. The entire train car chanted:

Ten!
Nine!
Eight!
Seven!
Six!
Five!
Four!
Three!

Two!
One!
HAPPY NEW YEAR!

Streamers flew, paper horns blew, and a champagne cork went

POP!

(Even though it was Prohibition, and booze had been illegal since before I was born, people still managed to always have it for special occasions. And not-so-special ones too, come to think of it.)

"Welcome 1932!" someone toasted. "You just *gotta* be better than 1931!"

"Hear hear!" everyone said.

After some celebrating, the conductor came through and loudly announced it was time to quiet down. "Lights out in five minutes!"

Soon after, everyone on board had fallen asleep. Including me.

But in the middle of the night, I woke up to the sound of someone crying.

I looked over at the Cruel. Asleep. I should've known it couldn't be her.

The Know-It-All and Goody-Two-Shoes were both passed out too, so I got up to have a look at the other two.

The Rude was not only asleep, he was drooling out of

his mouth, and his nose was making horrible sounds. He was disgusting even when he was unconscious.

The Hooligan was leaning against the window, his face buried into his coat. I thought he was asleep too, but no—*he* was the one crying.

"Hey," I said, touching his shoulder. "Hey, what's wrong?"

"*Nuttin!* Shuddup!" he said. "Go away!"

"No, seriously—what is it?" I whispered. "I won't tell anyone."

"You better not, or I'll pound you!" he said, and looked toward me long enough to shake a fist in my direction. He was holding his rabbit's foot in it.

His face and eyes were red and watery.

"Look, I cry all the time," I said. "It's no big deal."

"That's because you're a sissy."

I wanted to tell him I was lying—because I *was*—but I wanted to know why he was crying more than I wanted to set the record straight on how often *I* cried.

"It's because I ain't never been away from home before!" he said, snapping. "O.K.? You happy now? So **I'm** a big sissy, too!"

I told him I hadn't ever been away from home either.

"Are you lying?" he said.

"Absolutely not."

But I was.

It was still the middle of the night when we switched trains in New York. We had hours to wait, so I lay down on the platform and went to sleep.

I woke up to a kick in the ribs.

"C'mon!" the Rude said. "Train's comin'!"

It was morning. We got on the train with another long ride ahead of us, after which we would have to switch *again*. By tonight, we'd be in Quebec City, where we'd get to sleep in a hotel. I'd never slept in a hotel before, and the Brat had promised to put us up at the Ritz! "It's the only place my family *ever* stays."

(I was just worried we'd have to do the dishes or stay in the bathroom or something.)

I *again* got stuck next to the Cruel. So as not to accidentally break her invisible wall of death, I stood up in the aisle so I could talk to the others.

The Know-It-All and Goody-Two-Shoes, unfortunately, only wanted to talk about boring stuff. They were as bad as grown-ups. The Know-It-All also had made handwritten copies of the magazine article for us to read and study. Again: There should be *no studying* when you're running away from home!

Thankfully, the Rude and the Hooligan were into interesting stuff, like baseball, boxing, horse racing, and movies.

We spent hours talking about who was the best hit-ter, the strongest puncher, the fastest horse, and the scariest monster.

I picked the best one, of course—Mr. Hyde—while the Rude picked Dracula, and the Hooligan said Frankenstein.

"Is that because you *look* like Frankenstein?" the Cruel said.

"*Ooooooh*—crusted!" the Rude said, and laughed.

The Hooligan punched him in the arm.

When we got bored of all that, we did ten thousand rounds of "My Name Is Yon Yonson." It went:

"My name is Yon Yonson, I live in Wisconsin. I work in a lumberyard there. The people I meet as I walk down the street say, 'Hello!' I say, 'Hello!' They say, 'What's your name?' I say: 'My name is Yon Yonson, I live in Wisconsin. I work in a lumberyard there.' The people I meet as I walk down the street say, 'Hello!' I say, 'Hello!' They say, 'What's your name?' I say: 'My name is Yon Yonson, I live in Wisconsin. I work in a lumberyard there.' The people I meet as I walk down the street say, 'Hello!' I say, 'Hello!' They say, 'What's your name?' I say: 'My name is Yon Yonson, I live in Wisconsin. I work in a lumberyard there.' The people I meet as I walk down the street say, 'Hello!' I say, 'Hello!' They say, 'What's your name?' I say: 'My name is Yon Yon-

son, I live in Wisconsin. I work in a lumberyard there.' The people I meet as I walk down the street say, 'Hello!' I say, 'Hello!' They say, 'What's your name?' I say: 'My name is Yon Yonson, I live in Wisconsin. I work in a lumberyard there.' The people I meet as I walk down the street say, 'Hello!' I say, 'Hello!' They say, 'What's your name?' I say: 'My name is Yon Yonson, I live in Wisconsin. I work in a lumberyard there.' The people I meet as I walk down the street say, 'Hello!' I say, 'Hello!' They say, 'What's your name?' I say: 'My name is Yon Yonson, I live in Wisconsin. I work in a lumberyard there.' The people I meet as I walk down the street say, 'Hello!' I say, 'Hello!' They say, 'What's your name?' I say: 'My name is Yon Yonson, I live in Wisconsin. I work in a lumberyard there.' The people I meet as I walk down the street say, 'Hello!' I say, 'Hello!' They say, 'What's your name?' I say: 'My name is Yon Yonson, I live in Wisconsin. I work in a lumberyard there.' The people I meet as I walk down the street say, 'Hello!' I say, 'Hello!' They say, 'What's your name?' I say: 'My name is Yon Yonson, I live in Wisconsin. I work in a lumberyard there.' The people I meet as I walk down the street say, 'Hello!' I say, 'Hello!' They say, 'What's your name?' I say: 'My name is Yon Yonson, I live in Wisconsin. I work in a lumberyard there.' The people I meet as I walk down the street say, 'Hello!' I say, 'Hello!' They say, 'What's your name?' I say: 'My name is Yon Yonson—'"

"SHUT **UP!**" the Cruel yelled.

The rest of the train car clapped.

"Were we being annoying?" the Rude said.

◆ ◆ ◆

The last train ride was the shortest, and worst. We had run out of things to talk about, and I just wanted to be off of trains!

Making it even worster, the Know-It-All spouted out facts about every stop the train made.

"Rochester! Home of George Eastman and Eastman Kodak, which he f-f-f-founded. He is the inventor of the modern camera, and one of the nation's greatest philanthropists, b-b-b-being currently involved in establishing a new worldwide calendar with thirteen months."

"Do you have to make *everything* seem like school?" the Hooligan said.

My thoughts exactly.

But he didn't stop.

When we crossed the border into Canada—my first time in a foreign country!—the Know-It-All ruined the moment with a lesson on the history of Prohibition in Quebec.

"Because alcohol is legal in the province and city of Quebec, it is a popular base for smuggling. This has led to the rise of v-v-vicious criminal rings operated by bootleggers and rumrunners. In fact, the entire rise of the Syndicate and organized crime in America is largely tied to this illegal cross-border l-l-liquor trade."

"We know, we know!" we said.

Like we didn't watch the movies or listen to the radio? Heck, it was hard to be *alive* in 1931—er, 1932—and not know all about Lucky Luciano, Bugsy Siegel, and—the baddest gangster of them all—Al Capone.

FINALLY we heard the conductor say the words we had all been waiting for:

"Next stop! Quebec City!"

"Quebec City was settled by the French in—"

"Aw, shuddup!" the Hooligan said.

The Brat was waiting with his trunk on the platform when we got off.

"How was it back there with the cows and the luggage?" the Brat said. "Hah!"

"How was it up in first class with the *jerks*?" the Hooligan said. He looked around to see if anyone was laughing at his joke.

We were not.

It was then that I noticed something very strange. The people here—it was like they didn't know how to talk!

"They're speaking *French*," the Know-It-All said.

I had no clue they spoke French here, but not only did the Know-It-All know, he had prepared a list of questions in French along with the likely responses he would receive.

Armed with index cards, he tried getting us a taxi.

It didn't go so well.

Whatever he said sure sounded like French to *me*, but none of the taxi drivers seemed to have a clue what he was saying, and he didn't understand their responses back.

"None of their answers m-m-m-match my cards," he said, flipping through them.

The station was starting to get deserted, and we were starting to get nervous. We definitely didn't want to spend the night *here*. It was freezing, and a little bit scary.

The Know-It-All kept at it, until

"They don't speak that kind of French," a voice said.

The voice was coming from a tramp-looking boy, about our age. Except he wasn't a boy—she was a girl.

She was *dressed* like a boy, with long pants and suspenders and a hobo cap like the Rude wore. But she had a thick braid of black hair that hung like a rope down her back and she was *definitely* a girl.

"Not that it matters," she said. "No taxi's going to take seven kids anyway. But I will!"

What did she mean, *she* would?

14. PUTTIN' ON THE RITZ

"What do you mean, *you* will?" the Brat said.

"I can take you to your hotel," the tramp-girl said.

"*You* can drive?" the Brat said.

"Look who's talking," I said.

"Of course I can drive!" she said. "I've been driving for years! I've got a delivery truck parked right out back."

The Brat asked why she had a delivery truck.

"To make deliveries!" she said. "It's for the family . . . business."

We huddled to talk it over.

"What's to talk?" the Brat said. "What choice do we have?"

"But c-c-can we trust her?" the Know-It-All said.

"What's to *trust*?" the Brat said. "There's seven of us and only one of her!"

The tramp-girl was so eager to help, she even dragged the Brat's trunk out of the station and into the freezing cold—all by herself!

I do have to say I got a little nervous as we walked into the alley behind the station. It was dark and dodgy.

"How come you speak such g-g-good English?" the Know-It-All asked as we walked.

"Because I'm not from Quebec," she said. "How come a bunch of American kids are up here all alone?"

"We're traveling circus performers," I said.

I'd always wanted to be a traveling circus performer.

"There it is," she said.

On the side of the truck was a faded sign that read

MUMMY RUMMY'S
HOME-BAKED YUMMIES

"Is your family in the baking business?" Goody-Two-Shoes asked.

"What?" she said. "Oh yeah. *That's* what we are. In the *baking* business."

The Brat asked how much it was going to cost, and the tramp-girl asked which hotel she was taking us to.

"The *Ritz*?" she said. "The circus pays well!" The tramp-girl smiled and rubbed her chin. "The ride there will cost . . . let's say . . . five American dollars?"

"**Five** dollars!" the Brat said. "That's robbery!"

"Hey, it costs extra for the all of you!"

"Why does it cost extra?" the Brat said. "It's the same size truck!"

Once again, we didn't have much choice.

The tramp-girl opened the back of the truck for us to get in. There were no windows and it reeked of something rotten. I wasn't sure what, but it made me cough.

"Nothing to be afraid of!" she said.

It felt like we were being kidnapped. The Know-It-All was getting his barf-of-terror look, and I didn't have such a good feeling about it, either.

"You poor kids can all sit in the back," the Brat said. "I'm riding up front."

"That's not fair!" we all said, and the Brat reminded us yet again that *he* was the one who was paying.

The tramp-girl shrugged. "I do what the guy with the money says."

Thinking fast, I mentioned that I suffered from terminal claustrophobia. "It means I can die by being locked in a small space," I said, and hopped out of the back.

"Hey! I got that too! Thermal cost-a-whatsis!" the Rude said as the tramp-girl shut the doors on them and locked the back.

I breathed a sigh of relief as I settled into the middle seat up front.

"My name is Pearl," the tramp-girl said, getting in. "What's the name of your circus troupe?"

"The No-Good Nine," I said.

"The No-Good Nine?" she said. "But there are only seven of you!"

◆ ◆ ◆

As the tramp-girl drove her rickety truck over the bumpy cobblestones that passed for streets in this town, my teeth chattered like a rattle from all the vibrating. It was sweet relief when the ride finally ended.

Pearl pulled right up to the entrance of the Ritz and went around back to let the others out.

The Rude whistled. "Woo-wee! Ain't *this* the fanciest joint I ever seen!"

"It looks like a palace," Goody-Two-Shoes said.

"*Merci beaucoup!*" the tramp-girl said as the Brat counted out dollar bills. "That means thank you very much."

"*That* much French I know," he grumbled.

The tramp-girl helped us inside with the Brat's trunk, and stayed with the others while the Brat, the Know-It-All, and I went to the front desk.

The Brat asked for two rooms.

"I am so sorry, *monsieur*, but the hotel is booked," the man at the desk said.

"What?" the Brat said.

The clerk explained how there were no rooms, but the Brat wouldn't accept it.

"Do you have any idea who my father is?" he said. "Why, I could have him buy this rathole and **fire** you!" It didn't help.

"Full is full," the clerk said.

Then the tantrum thing happened, with the Brat's face turning as red as the cherry on top of a sundae.

That didn't help, either.

"Maybe you could tell us where another hotel is?" I asked.

"*What* other hotel, *monsieur*? It is New Year's Day!" The clerk threw up his hands. "All the hotels are filled with Americans who want to drink champagne without worrying about getting arrested!"

I said we didn't need anything fancy—just a flophouse with a few beds—but the clerk said he was sure he wouldn't know of such a place.

Did I mention he was real snooty?

The Know-It-All asked if there might be rooms to rent near the docks. "We have to take the 9:35 a.m. boat in the m-m-morning."

The clerk raised an eyebrow.

"The *docks*?" he said. "The docks are closed for the winter."

"What do you mean?" the Know-It-All said. "I have the b-b-b-boat schedule right here!"

The manager looked at it and pointed to the words *été seulement*.

"That means 'summer only,'" he said. "The river is frozen until May."

The Know-It-All had his worst case of barf-face yet when we went back to where the others were waiting.

"How did that go for you?" the tramp-girl said.

The Know-It-All went from green to greener.

"He screwed it all up, that's how it went!" the Brat

said. "There aren't any ships until JUNE!"

"*June?*" the Cruel said.

"Some Know-It-All *you* turned out to be!" the Rude said.

"What are we gonna do now?" the Hooligan said. "We'll never get to Santa's!"

"To *Santa's?*" the tramp-girl said. "You are performing the circus for Santa?"

"There's nothing we can do about it tonight," Goody-Two-Shoes said, picking up her bag. "So where's our room?"

The Brat, the Know-It-All, and I looked at each other and shrugged.

The Cruel let out a *Puh!* of disgust. "You three really are a bunch of ignoramuses."

"Wait, there's no *room?*" the Rude said. "Where are we gonna sleep?"

"*I* know where you can go," the tramp-girl said smiling. "And it won't even cost you a dime!"

◆ ◆ ◆

Meanwhile . . .

The Truant Officer and the Vainglorious—remember those two? When last we saw them, they were on that train platform back in Pittsburgh.

Now, I can't tell you what happened to them for sure, because I wasn't there. However, I do have in my possession further journals of my archenemy, who—let's face it—is way more accurate about reporting stuff than I am.

From his diary of that night, as translated by someone who knows Russian a heckuva lot better than me:

> The boy that I captured has been able to provide information that is helping me piece together something about the plans and whereabouts of the child conspirators, a.k.a. "the No-Good Nine." This boy is, however, problematic.
>
> For one thing, he seems to be of below-average intelligence.
>
> As an example, he believes that his being left by the others was some sort of mistake.
>
> BOY: "The No-Good Nine are my best friends, so they couldn't have meant for me to get left behind! They must be really worried about me."
>
> The child seems unable to understand that they tricked him.
>
> He tells me that the No-Good Nine are headed to Quebec City, but will not divulge where they will be staying or where they are going afterward unless I take him with me.
>
> I tell him that this is impossible, that I

need to get him to his parents, but he refuses to reveal his name. He insists that I call him "Glorious," like all of his friends do.

I fear he is mentally unstable.

A decision must be made: I can take him to the police station, or bring him with me in search of the No-Good Nine.

Now, you might be asking yourself, would a truant officer *really* take a child out of the country? Since that might be considered, y'know, *kidnapping*.

For any normal catcher of school-skipping kids the answer would be NO. But my nemesis was no normal anything.

Ivan Ivanovich, former secret agent of the tsar, had a dream. He wanted to become a real police officer, and in his mind, breaking up a criminal gang of children bent on ruining Christmas would be just the thing to get him the job.

So he took the Vainglorious with him to Quebec. In fact, they were coming on the next train.

"NEXT STOP! ROCHESTER!" the conductor calls.

15. MUMMY RUMMY

Rattle-rumble-bump the truck barreled through the narrow, winding streets, and it was hard to keep my teeth from knocking into each other, and my butt on the seat. So I was thankful when the tramp-girl slowed down the truck and pulled over behind another truck. It was the same model and also had *Mummy Rummy's Home-Baked Yummies* written across the side.

"Is that who we're going to stay with?" I said. "Mummy Rummy?"

The tramp-girl nodded yes.

"Her name is Rummy Renée, but everyone calls her Mummy."

It had to be past midnight by now, and the sky was a swirling stew of clouds and moon and stars. It all felt a little threatening as we followed the tramp-girl down a set of half-broken stairs that led from the street to a seedy area by the port.

"Are we *sure* this is a good idea?" the Know-It-All whispered to me and the Brat.

"Don't be such a chicken all the time!" the Brat said.

From up ahead, the tramp-girl pointed. "There it is," she said. "Home."

"Home" was a shack that leaned all the more with each gust of wind. A light flickered in the window, and smoke ran out of a tin pipe that poked out of the roof like a little top hat.

"At least it's *heated*," the Hooligan said, rubbing his hands together.

We followed the tramp-girl inside, where we found three people playing cards at a table, a pile of funny-looking coins in the middle. The two facing us were teenagers, the one on the left all skinny with an Adam's apple like a rooster's wattle. The other one was more of a bruiser and had a single black eyebrow that went straight across his forehead.

The third one was a lady. A BIG lady. She had her back to us, and boy, was it a *lot* of back—like a mountain.

The two teenagers silently looked up at us from their cards but kept on playing.

Meanwhile, the tramp-girl went to the lady and said something. It was in French, so who knows what the heck it was. The lady said something back in a voice as loud as a sawmill.

Then she turned around.

The thick cigar was unusual enough—I'd never seen a woman smoke a stogie before—but what really surprised me was that when she smiled, you could see that she had a gold tooth.

I had a moment of fear—the kind of fear where you

want to run away but your whole body freezes. Then the gold-toothed lady let out a big, hearty laugh and got up to give us all hugs.

My momma was so thin and bony, it hurt when she hugged you, but with this lady, it was like a mattress wrapping around you.

"*Bienvenue!* Well-*come!* Well-*come!*" she said in a thick accent. "I am Rummy Renée, but call me *Mummy!* Everyone does—isn't that right, sonny-boys?"

The other two poker players nodded their heads, and both said, "*Oui*, Mummy."

"They don't speak English," the tramp-girl said.

She told us they were her brothers, which was weird, since neither of them looked anything like her, or each other. The other weird thing was that they were both named Jack. The skinny brother was Rooster Jack and the thug-looking one was Black Jack.

"My daughter says you are stuck on this freezing-cold night with nowhere to stay. Well, you are in luck, because my 'ome is your 'ome!!" Mummy said. "Make yourselves comfortable! And tell your Mummy—why is it you 'ave come to Quebec?"

"We're going to Labrador," the Brat said. "There's a magical lighthouse there that—"

"No! No we're n-n-n-not," the Know-It-All said, cutting him off.

The Brat looked annoyed at the Know-It-All, who

obviously didn't trust Mummy. But how *could* you trust someone named Mummy Rummy? (Not to mention a pair of brothers named Jack.)

"What he means is we *are* going to a lighthouse," I said, "and that it's *like* magic. Because aren't *all* lighthouses like magic?"

"And *why* are you going to this magic-not-magic light'ouse?" Mummy said.

"We're orphan circus performers," I said. "And we're doing a tour of the coast to give lonely lighthouse keepers a little entertainment."

"Wait," the Hooligan said. "We're gonna have to *perform*?"

The Rude elbowed him in the gut.

"I am sure I can 'elp you get to this light'ouse," Mummy said. "I am in the transportation business, after all. You know, for my . . . products."

"How much will you charge?" the Brat asked suspiciously.

Mummy exhaled a cloud of cigar smoke like she was blowing away the very idea.

"Ah, I would not *dream* of profiting a penny. I love to 'elp the orphans! Isn't that right, Pearl?" She looked at the tramp-girl.

"Can I ask you a question, Mummy?" Goody-Two-Shoes said.

"Certainly, *ma chérie!*"

"Why are you called Mummy *Rummy*?"

Mummy laughed her explosive laugh. "Why else? I am a *rumrunner*!"

That gave us all a reason to think twice.

"W-w-why do your trucks say you're a baker?" the Know-It-All asked.

"Ah, but I *am* a baker," she said. "'Ere, try one." She opened a tin of biscuits and held it out for us to try.

"Me first!" the Rude said. "I'm starvin'!" But as soon as he took a bite, he looked like he regretted it.

I took a nibble of one and it tasted absolutely

"Terrible, yes?"

Mummy snapped the tin shut, shaking her head. "No one ever buys them, so I 'ad to try a different line of work," she said. "And it winds up that selling booze is much more profitable than selling biscuits!"

"Are you *really* a bootlegger?" the Rude said. "That's so jake!"

I thought it was swell too—a real rumrunner!—but I could tell Goody-Two-Shoes was horrified. And so was the Know-It-All.

"I never heard of a *woman* rumrunner before," the Brat said skeptically.

The happy eyes of Mummy suddenly narrowed to slits. She blew a cloud of smoke into the Brat's face.

"Yes," she said. "It is not *usual* to find a woman in such a man's line of work. Not easy, either! There is much to overcome. I tell little Pearl all the time—we are women, we have to be *twice* as tough as the men. Isn't that right, Pearlie?"

"Yes, Mummy."

"And twice as mean," the Cruel muttered.

"Good girl!" Mummy said, smiling at the Cruel.

"Instead of being twice as tough and mean, maybe we should be twice as gentle and kind," Goody-Two-Shoes said.

"Ah-ah!" Mummy tossed her head back to guffaw. "The only thing men understand is this."

She tapped on her gold tooth.

"And this."

She pulled a knife out from under the table.

Which was a pretty neat trick, if not a little terrifying. For the Know-It-All especially.

"So you're a c-c-c-c . . ."

He had trouble spitting out the word.

". . . *criminal?*"

"A criminal! No!" Mummy placed her big ham hands on his shoulders. "Rum and liquor—they are not illegal 'ere in Quebec! Even children drink them! You must try some! Let us toast in the 'appy New Year!"

One of the Brothers Jack smiled, making me wonder if they didn't know a little more English than they let on.

Mummy grabbed a bottle off a shelf and pulled out its

cork. The liquid inside was foggy, and she poured a glass for each Naughty Lister. That bottle empty, she pulled out another and poured glasses for herself and her three children.

"To new friends!" Mummy said, raising her glass. She then tossed it back in one go, as did the tramp-girl and the Brothers Jack.

I looked into my glass, then to the other No-Good Ninesters.

"Try it!" Mummy said, pouring herself another.

"What are you?" the tramp-girl said, turning to the Brat. "*Afraid?*"

The Brat repeated the word *afraid* like it was absurd, and took a big gulp of whatever was in the glass.

He spit it right back out.

Everyone laughed.

The Hooligan, the Rude, and the Cruel all tried it too—or pretended to, like I did. I'd been around plenty of alcohol (my uncle Peppe made grappa in his bathtub back home), but it didn't look—or *smell*—anything like this. One whiff made me go all queasy.

The Know-It-All, on the other hand, wasn't even pretending. He treated his glass like it was liquid dynamite.

"It may not be illegal to have l-l-l-liquor here," he said. "But it *is* illegal to bring it into the US."

"Ah, right you are!" Mummy said. "You are not a

customs officer, are you? Please don't shoot!" She held up both hands with a frightened look on her face, then burst into laughter again.

She downed another glass in one gulp, wiped her mouth on her sleeve, and said, "Now 'oo wants to play poker?"

"We're so lucky we found you, Mummy!" the Hooligan said as we sat down at the table.

Only Goody and the Know-It-All didn't hang around the card table. They were off in the corner whispering.

When Mummy went to use the outhouse, the Know-It-All dragged me and the Brat away from the others.

"I'm telling you, there's something *wr-r-rong* here!"

"Wrong? What could be wrong?" the Brat said.

"M-M-M-Mummy is a rumrunner!" he said. "That's wrong enough!"

"So?" the Brat said. "She's like us. Naughty and no good."

I didn't remember seeing any Bootleggers or Smugglers on the Naughty List, but he had a point.

"Well, what about the t-t-t-tramp-girl and the two brothers?" the Know-It-All said. "I think they're *all* c-c-c-criminals. And that knife!"

"They're not criminals, they're bootleggers," the Brat said. "It's different! I say they're on the level. And I should know—I'm an *excellent* judge of character."

Except, it wound up, he wasn't.

16. THIEVES THAT GO BUMP IN THE NIGHT

I have no idea what time the night ended. It got to be hard to keep my eyes open and then they were burning from the cigar smoke, so I lay down on the floor and as soon as I did, I fell asleep.

The night didn't end, however—at least not with falling asleep. Because it was still night when I woke up.

I had to pee!

But it was *so* dark, I couldn't see anything but a bunch of dark lumps on the floor. My fellow No-Good Ninesters.

Then I heard

Creeeeeak!

Peering through the dark I saw another figure, but this one wasn't a lump. It was standing up. And now it was kneeling. And opening something.

The lid on the Brat's trunk.

Someone was going through his stuff! Someone—maybe—who knew he kept a whole lot of silver in there.

At first I thought it was the Hooligan—I mean, he *was* in a gang—but this person wasn't that big. Then I thought the Rude, because of the cap. But I could hear the Rude snoring. (*Geez* could he snore!)

As it turned out, it wasn't any of *us*.

It was Pearl—the tramp-girl.

"Stop!" I yelled. "Thief!"

The tramp-girl was startled and dropped what she was holding.

Silver coins went plinking and clanking and rolling across the floor.

Now everyone woke up. Including the kid all that silver belonged to.

"*Thief?*" the Brat said. "What—*who*—where?"

"I can explain!" the tramp-girl said, throwing up her arms.

The Brat scrambled to his feet and made a move to grab her, but she head-butted him and bolted away.

"I got her!" the Hooligan said.

But who he had was the Rude. "Get yer meathooks off a me, ya big oaf!"

"She's over there!" Goody-Two-Shoes yelled.

The tramp-girl was racing for the door, right where the Cruel now stood.

The Cruel tackled her, and the tramp-girl hit the floor face-first, but came up swinging and caught the Cruel with a fist to the jaw.

"That **hurt**!" the Cruel said. Angry, she forced the thief to the ground and pinned her arms down with her knees, and then

BOOM!

The door slammed open.

A kerosene lamp lit the room, swinging from the outstretched arm of Mummy Rummy.

The yellow-red fire lit her face from below, which was kind of scary. So was the knife she was holding in the other hand.

"Mummy!" the Brat said. "Thank god you're here. Your daughter was stealing my money!"

"She was *what*?" Mummy said. Her face turned furious. "She was *stealing* from you? *My* daughter? Now, what 'ave I told you about that, dear daughter?"

The Cruel got up off Pearl as Mummy took a few steps toward them, her lamp shining off the coins scattered all over the floor. Boy, were there a *lot* of coins.

"There's more too!" the tramp-girl said. "Lots more— inside the trunk! I can show you!"

I gotta admit, I was confused. The tramp-girl was a thief—that was for sure. But was Mummy a crook, too?

Mummy walked over to her and knelt down. The tramp-girl was nursing a fat lip from the scuffle.

"Let me see that," Mummy said, and lifted the thief's face up by the chin.

Then

PUNCH!

Mummy hit her square in the face with the hilt of the knife and sent the tramp-girl reeling across the room. She went smack against the wall.

"You *tabarnouche* of a child!" Mummy said. "You think you can rob these Americans without me? Were you going to run away with the money? With *this* money!" Mummy sent a bunch of silver coins flying with a kick.

Then she turned toward *us*.

"Now, you American children listen to me and you listen to me good!" she said, shaking the point of the knife at us. "You tell me what I want to know, *comprenez?* And if you tell me more lies, I swear you will wish I only beat you as bad as 'er!" She spit in the direction of Pearl.

Her daughter.

"*You* start!" Mummy said, pointing her knife at the Brat. "Or do you need more of that poison I gave you?"

"That wasn't rum?" the Brat said.

"Hah! I wouldn't waste my rum on you! That was water and gasoline!" Mummy went over to the Brat and pressed the tip of the knife to the tip of the Brat's nose. "Now *talk*."

It was amazing—even with a knife in his face, the Brat was still a brat. A temper tantrum rose right up into his ripening face.

"This is an *outrage*! You are just as bad as your daughter! Why, *you* probably taught her to steal," he said. "We'll call the authorities and then you'll be sorry. **Real** sorry!"

Mummy grabbed the Brat by the hair—the long flap on top of his head that he took such care to mold into place—and jerked him up

"OW!"

Then she took her knife and sawed that chunk of hair right off, giving him an instant flattop.

I might have laughed. If I hadn't been the most terrified I'd ever been in my entire life, that is.

"Now, if you don't want this to be your 'ead," Mummy said, wagging the sliced-off hair in front of the Brat's face like a dead muskrat, "*talk!*"

For the first time—maybe in his life—the Brat had a temper tantrum snuffed out. The red dropped right down his face, leaving his skin as white as a ghost.

"What-what-what," the Brat stammered. "What do you want to know?"

"**EVERYTHING!**" Mummy shouted so loud, her voice shook the walls of the shack.

It was at that moment that someone peed their pants.

It was *not* me.

I swear.

"'**Oo** are you supposed to meet?!" Mummy shouted, tapping the Brat's nose with the knife.

"What do you mean—*who*?" he said.

"You think I believe you are in a circus! You think Mummy Rummy is a *fool*!" she shouted, and banged the hilt of her knife against the wall behind the Brat, putting a hole in it. "I *know* why you came to Quebec! American bootleggers 'ave sent you. You could buy 'alf the liquor in Canada with all the silver you 'ave in 'ere!"

It sounds crazy, right? That Mummy thought *we* were rumrunners, too? But the thing is, bootleggers and rumrunners used kids to commit crimes all the time. Because if a kid got caught, they'd only get sent to re-form school. If an adult got arrested, they'd get twenty years in the pen. So *she* thought some American gangsters had sent us here to make a buy. Besides—how else would we have gotten a trunk full of silver?

" '**Oo** is it you are supposed to buy the liquor from? Is it Monkey Paul? Is it Stumps McCoy?" Mummy stabbed the table with each name

POK!

POK!

"*Non!* I know 'oo it is!" she said. "Frère Balzac! That pig!"

I looked at the Hooligan and the Rude. They were both as confused as me.

"*Now* tell me 'oo sent you! Was it the Syndicate?" Mummy said. "No, wait—with this much money, it 'ad to be Capone! *Tell* me it was Capone!"

"Capone! *Al* Capone?" the Brat said, frantic. "No! It's not like you think! No one sent us!"

"You *do* think Mummy is a fool!!" she yelled, pressing her knife to the Brat's throat. "I will show you 'oo is the fool! Now **TELL ME**!"

"Tell her! Tell her why we're here!" the Brat said to the Know-It-All.

"Me? Why *m-m-m-m-m-me*?"

Mummy turned to the Know-It-All, and as soon as she pointed the knife in his direction, it all spilled out of him.

About us getting coal in our stockings. About him finding the Naughty List. About how we wanted to play with the toys of the Nice kids of the world. About the article that had the interview with the lighthouse keeper. About how we were gonna signal Santa with Morse code. About how a magical narwhal would arrive with a golden barge and whisk us off to the North Pole. About how all the houses in Santaland looked like they were made of gingerbread. About—

The Know-It-All stopped.

Mummy's eyes had turned from angry slits to wide-open circles of amazement. Then she burst into laughter.

"That! *That* is the best story I 'ave ever 'eard!" Mummy said. Tears filled her eyes and she slapped her thigh, again and again. "A light'ouse! Morse code to Santa! And the narwhal—oh, *mon dieu*, not the magical narwhal! *AH-AH-AH!*"

I turned to the Know-It-All—all of us did. His face was red with shame.

It suddenly occurred to me, as Mummy sat there

laughing—it *did* sound like a stupid plan. And I *still* didn't know what the heck a narwhal was.

"You want to go to Santaland, children?" Mummy said. "Oh, I will send you *right* to Santaland!"

17. A TURN FOR THE WORSE

Y'know, I kinda shoulda hated Pearl the tramp-girl thief. I mean, she *was* the reason we had gotten into this mess. If it wasn't for her, we'd have still had the silver and not been trapped with a maniacal gold-toothed bootlegger lady holding a knife on us.

But what Mummy was about to do to her—well, it was awful. *Scary* awful. The tramp-looking girl might've been a thief, but she didn't deserve *this*.

Pearl's eye was puffed and turning black from where Mummy had hit her, but that wasn't the awful part. The awful part came when Mummy opened a trapdoor in the floor.

You would never have noticed it, but once Mummy opened it, it was like she had opened a door to hell.

You always think of hell as this really warm place full of flames, but in that moment I knew it wasn't like that at all. It was like *this*—a hole in the ground that opened to nothing but darkness and cold and had the smell of mold and rot.

"Please, Mummy! Don't!" the tramp-girl begged, but Mummy Rummy had no pity.

She grabbed her daughter and shoved the girl down into the shallow pit, giving her a hard push to the back that landed her somewhere down in the darkness with a

THUD!

Then Mummy kicked the trapdoor shut.

"I will deal with *you* later!" she said.

Then Mummy told the Hooligan and the Rude to move the Brat's chest over the trapdoor, but it was so heavy—and they were so scared—they had trouble pushing it.

"*Tabarnouche!*" Mummy shouted. "American weaklings!" With one kick of her boot, the chest went shooting across the floor.

Mummy's sonny-boys—Rooster Jack and Black Jack—were there now too, and they didn't lift a finger to help their little sister. In fact, they were grinning at her banging and pleading like it was hilarious. What a couple of jerks! Worse than jerks. My big brothers were capital-J Jerks, and even they wouldn't have left me trapped under a *floor*!

This was some kind of family. And if they had done this to their own flesh and blood, what the heck were they gonna do to *us*?

The Brothers Jack herded us outside and marched

us up the rickety steps to the street. They put us in the back of one of the trucks and

CLANCK!

loudly locked the doors shut.

It was pitch-black, and now *we* were the ones trapped. Even though we had each other, I didn't like our chances any better than the tramp-girl's.

The engine came spitting—rumbling—roaring to life, and the truck took off. It was even bouncier in the back, and noisier, with empty liquor bottles jangling and clinking and jumping around.

The Know-It-All was squatting clutching his brief-case, which—along with Goody-Two-Shoes's sewing kit—was all that any of us had managed to take.

"*What are we g-g-g-going to do do?*" he said, whispering.

"*Where are they taking us?*" Goody said, also whispering.

"Why are you **WHISPERING**?" the Cruel said loudly. "They can't hear us with that engine! We can barely hear **ourselves!**"

"She seemed like such a *nice* lady. . . ." the Hooligan said. "She reminded me of my momma. My *momma . . .*"

His eyes started to tear up.

"Oh *brother*," the Cruel said.

No one talked for a while. The Hooligan pulled himself together, then started sniffing. I thought it was from the crying, but he was sniffing *me*.

"What are you, a dog?" I said.

"You smell like *pee*," he said.

"That's not me!" I whispered. "*I think it's the Rude!*"

Which was a good person to blame it on, since he always smelled like *something*.

The truck must have hit a rock, because it suddenly went tilting over to one side, knocking me right into the Hooligan.

"Oh *gross!*" he said. "The Liar touched me! Now I got his pee on me!"

"Shouldn't we really be talking about something else?" I said. "Like how we're all about to die?"

That got everyone real quiet again.

The ride was long and rough, and only got longer and rougher. It felt like we weren't even on a real road anymore, and the bottles got so knocked around that a few of them smashed, and we were all banging into each other too. It was terrible and terrifying. But what was worse was when it all went still. And silent.

"Are we stopped?" the Rude said.

"*Yes, we're stopped!*" the Cruel whispered. "*And **now** you should whisper.*"

We heard footsteps and

CLANCK!

someone unlocked the rear gate of the truck. It swung open to the *blinding* morning sun. The snow everywhere made it worse—it was like we were *on* the sun—and the hurt in my eyes shot straight into my brain.

When my eyes finally adjusted, I saw Mummy and her sonnies. They were holding tommy guns.

Gulp.

18. WHERE IT ALL FALLS APART

Do you know what a tommy gun is? It's the kind of gun that fires bullets

bapbapbapbapbapbap

all in a row, without the gunman ever having to take his—or her—finger off the trigger. It was the favorite weapon of bootleggers, gangsters, and rumrunners.

Mummy waved her gun for us to start walking, and she and her sonny-boys herded us into the middle of the open, snowy field. It was like standing on an empty sheet of paper you couldn't see the end of.

Was this *it*?

Were they going to kill us? And leave our dead bodies out here in the middle of the snowy nowhere?

It was kind of hard to see at that moment what else they might be planning.

Mummy smiled—her gold tooth glistening in the sun—and

"Pop! Pop! Pop!"

I closed my eyes—this *was* it!

But . . . it wasn't.

I was still alive.

She hadn't even fired the gun. (But she'd done an *awfully* good imitation.)

"AH-AH-AH!" she laughed at us flinching and covering ourselves.

"Never say Mummy didn't give you a sporting chance," she said, and pointed with the tommy gun in the direction of the truck. "Quebec is forty miles back *that* way—*if* you can find the way!" she said. "If any of you manage to make it back alive, I'll be impressed. And 'ere's this—" she said, flinging a tin of *Mummy Rummy's Home-Baked Yummies* at us. The top popped off, and biscuits skidded across the crusted-over snow. "In case you get 'ungry! *AH-AH-AH!*"

Still laughing her evil laugh—I think it's fair to call it evil—she and the Jacks got back into the truck, shut the door

SLAM!

turned on the motor, and sped off, leaving a trail of black smoke and tire tracks.

We kept watching until the truck was out of sight.

Then the Rude and the Hooligan descended upon the biscuits.

"These aren't so bad!" the Rude said, gnawing.

"Yeah, you just hafta make sure you don't bust a tooth," the Hooligan said.

"I can't believe you two can eat at a time like this!" Goody-Two-Shoes said. "What are we going to do?!"

"Well, if Mummy is right, and Quebec is forty miles that w-w-way," the Know-It-All said, "then it should take us thirteen hours and twenty minutes to get there, given the average human walking pace of three miles per hour. Considering the declination of the sun, I'd say we have r-r-roughly seven hours and thirty-six minutes of sunlight left, which means we will have five hours and forty-four minutes of walking in the dark to get back to the city."

"Are you *joking*?" the Cruel said.

"What?" the Know-It-All said. "Do you think my c-c-c-calculations are off?"

"I'm not talking about your *calculations*, Know-It-All," she said. "I'm talking about the idea that we are going to follow *you* anywhere!"

The Know-It-All's expression went meek.

"We were supposed to hop a ride to the North Pole aboard a magic *narwhal*?" the Cruel said. "**That** was your brilliant plan?"

"I told you about the n-n-n-narwhal," the Know-It-All said. "But none of you wanted to listen! You just wanted to talk about playing with toys and p-p-p-punching Santa!"

"I still don't know what a nar-wall even is!" the Hooligan said, making that two of us.

"It's a unicorn w-w-whale," the Know-It-All said.

"Hey, unicorns don't exist!" the Rude said.

"But narwhals do!" the Know-It-All said.

"*Magic* ones?" the Cruel said.

"But it's all true!" the Know-It-All said. "It was in a m-m-m-magazine!"

"And you think everything in a magazine is *true*?" the Cruel said. "If you do, then you're the biggest dope of us all!"

"*Wait*," the Hooligan whispered to me. "*Everything in a magazine isn't true?*"

"Look, you had a chance to change the p-p-plan if you didn't like it, but none of you wanted to even *listen* to it!" the Know-It-All said. "You were too busy trying to figure out if Frankenstein could b-b-b-beat up Dracula!"

"Hey, don't turn this around!" the Rude said.

"Yeah! We should've known not to trust you from the minute you screwed up the boat schedule!" the Brat said. "We should've gone home *then*!"

"Can everyone please stop?" Goody-Two-Shoes said. "Fighting isn't going to help us. We have to start walking back to the city."

"And *then* what?" the Brat said, his face turning tomato-soup red. "Even if we survive, we don't have any money left! That filthy rotten thief and her gold-toothed mother stole all my money!!"

"I kept *t-t-t-telling* you we shouldn't trust them," the Know-It-All said. "I t-t-t-**told** you! But you wouldn't l-l-listen! *You never listen!*"

"**NO ONE TALKS TO ME LIKE THAT!**" the Brat said, and made a flying tackle of the Know-It-All.

They both fell over in a heap in the snow.

"You dirty rotten B-B-B-**Brat**!" the Know-It-All hollered. "Get off of me!"

"**FIGHT FIGHT FIGHT!**" the Hooligan and the Rude chanted.

It was sad to see the two of them going at it. First, because they were almost friends. Second, because neither of them knew how to throw a punch.

I needed to stop it.

"Break it up! Break it up!" I shouted, getting in the middle of it. *Caught* in the middle of it, that is.

Because

POW!

right in *my* face.

"**OW!** Stop it!" I said. Then another punch hit me. "**OW!** Stop it, you chumps! And learn how to aim a punch!"

I started hitting back. What choice did I have?

"You're both jerks and it's *both* of your faults!" I yelled, whaling at them with both fists.

It felt good.

Pretty soon, all our energy and anger was spent, and the three of us lay on the ground, huffing and puffing in the pounded-down snow.

A long, sharp shadow came looming over us.

It was the Cruel.

"You three disgust me," she said. "I've seen better fighting from the kindergarten girls at Saint Hedwig's. But what *really* disgusts is me is that the only reason we are out here in the first place is that you three little boys didn't get a present on Christmas and that made you sad in your warm, snug homes in fancy-schmancy Sewickley. *Boo-hoo!* So you decided to lead us poor Pittsburghers on your adventure to Santaland, with your ***plans***"

(She turned to the Know-It-All.)

"and your ***money***"

(She turned to the Brat.)

"and your ***dumb*** names and passwords!"

(She turned to me.)

"*Our* mistake was letting you three be in charge," the Cruel said. "**NOT! ANY! MORE!**"

None of the three of us said a word. She did, after all, kind of have a point. (Except about the names and passwords.)

"I'm going *this* way," the Cruel said, turning away from me. "If any of the rest of you want to survive, I suggest you come with me."

The Cruel began walking in the tracks that Mummy's truck had left in the snow.

"I'm with her!" the Rude said, following.

"Me too!" the Hooligan said, right behind.

And I sure wasn't sticking around neither!

"Y'know, I was never really with those other two guys," I said. "And my home is *really* crappy!"

As for those other two guys . . .

"Come on," Goody-Two-Shoes said to the Brat and the Know-It-All, still nursing their wounds on the ground. "The *last* one I want to take orders from is the Cruel, but we need to stick together. Whether we like it or not."

19. A LONG COLD WALK IN WHEREVER THE HECK THIS IS

"Ouch!"

The Brat stopped and lifted up the sole of his shoe.

"I have a hole in my shoe," he said. "A literal *hole* in the bottom of my shoe! It hurts!"

"Stop whining, rich boy," the Cruel said. "Just keep moving!"

"You're lucky you're beautiful," the Brat said. "Or everyone would hate you."

"I'm sure no one's ever said that *you* are too beautiful to hate," the Cruel said.

The Rude sniggered. "That was a good one! Haw!"

The Cruel wasn't only picking on the Brat. She had been insulting all of us for hours. I think it was her idea of "motivation."

As for herself, she walked ramrod straight and didn't seem to feel the cold or pain or hunger. Or anything whatsoever.

Me, I felt everything. Cold, pain, hunger, and something else—something *really* uncomfortable. I began walking sort of bowlegged, and started to fall behind.

"What's wr-r-r-wrong with you?" the Know-It-All called back to me.

"I just like looking at the landscape," I said "Such beautiful . . . *uhhhh* . . . **snow**!"

"Do you have to go to the bathroom?" the Know-It-All said. "Why don't you just g-g-go?"

"I can't!" I said.

"Haw-haw!" the Rude said. "The Liar has to take a *crap*!"

"Oh, just do it and get it over with," the Cruel said, rolling her eyes.

I didn't want to, but I *had* to, so I started to unbuckle my pants and

"Go behind a **tree**, you idiot!" the Cruel yelled, pointing at the woods. "None of us want to watch!"

I fast rushed off behind a pine, unzipping my pants along the way, and I squatted down and

AHHHH!

When I was done, though, I realized I hadn't quite thought this through.

"Hey!" I hollered. "What am I supposed to use to *wipe*?!"

"The snow!" the Cruel hollered back.

It was *really* cold.

I had to run to catch back up with the others.

We had gotten to what seemed like an actual road, rather than just tracks in the snow. This was a good thing, and we hoped that a car would come passing and pick us up. But that wasn't happening.

And now it was starting to get dark. The wind picked up, bringing a whole new level of cold with it.

It was so miserable, no one was talking anymore. Except for the Rude, who *always* talked. It was like he couldn't think unless it was out loud. He was wondering how everybody was doing back at his boardinghouse, the boxing gym, and the track. He started talking about each horse and how much grain they got, and what kind of hay. He didn't care how many times the Cruel told him to shut up, he just kept on talking.

He was explaining how he mucked out the horses' stalls when he stopped and pointed up at the sky.

"Hey," he said. "What are *those* things?"

We all stopped and tried to figure out what he was looking at.

"You mean the *stars*?" the Know-It-All said.

"Oh, wow," the Rude said. "So *that's* what stars look like!"

"You're *k-k-kidding*, right?"

"I live in Pittsburgh," the Rude said, shrugging. "We're lucky if we see the *sun*!"

"That one star-thingie is HUGE," the Hooligan said, pointing at

"The moon?" The Know-It-All couldn't quite handle it. "Are you talking about the *moon*?"

"Yeah, the moon-thingie!" the Hooligan said. "Y'know, I think it even *moved*. It had been over there, and now it's over here!"

"That's what the m-m-moon *does*!"

On the horizon now was something brighter than the stars and moon. Two things, in fact.

Headlights.

There was a vehicle, and it was headed right at us. Finally!

We all jumped up and down screaming and waving for it to stop.

"We're saved!" Goody-Two-Shoes said.

"*If* it stops," the Cruel said.

It did stop. But that was the scariest thing of all.

Because it was a truck. And on its side, it read:

MUMMY RUMMY'S
HOME-BAKED YUMMIES

20. SURPRISE!

Had Mummy changed her mind and decided she *did* want to come back and kill us?

I probably should've run the other way—we all should have—but instead we just stood there like a bunch of lambs waiting for the farmer to get his ax.

The driver's-side door opened. I held my breath . . .

. . . and I let it out.

It was *not* Mummy who stepped out of the truck.

It was the tramp-girl!

"**YOU!**" the Brat shouted.

"Are all of you O.K.?" she said.

"Like you care!" the Brat yelled, throwing another fire-engine-red fit. "**Thief!** How dare you steal my money! If you weren't a girl, I'd knock your block off!"

"That," the Cruel said, "is not a problem *I* have."

She stepped in front of the Brat and

PUNCH!

socked the tramp-girl right in the kisser.

That looked like it *hurt*.

The girl put her hands to her nose. When she took them away, it was bleeding.

"I deserve that," she said.

"Can we please just *stop* with all the violence!" Goody-Two-Shoes said, pushing the Cruel away.

She then went up to the tramp-girl to see if she was all right, and asked, "Why are you here?"

But before she could open her mouth, the Brat said, "Mummy must've sent her! How else could she have escaped! There's no way she could have lifted up the trapdoor with my chest on top of it."

"I didn't have to," the tramp-girl said. "Mummy did the same thing to me once before, so I went and took the nails out of one of the floorboards in case she ever tried it again. I escaped after you left and stole her other truck."

"So your mother doesn't know you're here?" Goody said.

"If she did, she'd kill me. *Actually* kill me," the tramp-girl said. "And she's *not* my mother. Not my real one, anyway."

"Well, if she didn't send you," the Cruel said, "then why did you come looking for us?"

Pearl reached into her pocket and grabbed something to hold out for all of us to see.

A lump of coal.

"I'm a Naughty Lister," she said. "And I want to play with the toys of that *tabarnouche* Santa, too!"

21. AND THEN THERE WERE EIGHT

It was another long ride.

The Brat was sore at everybody and everything. He was mad at all his money being gone, mad at his precious hair being cut, mad about getting driven around by the thief-girl—even if she was saving our lives—and mad about the Cruel now being in charge. She even got to sit shotgun!

"Girls up front," the Cruel said. "Boys in the *back*."

While the truck rumbled along, us boys in the back discussed whether or not we thought the tramp-girl was on the level or if this was just another trick.

"But what would she *trick* us for?" I said. We didn't have any more money, and what possible gain could she get from saving our lives?

The facts, however, didn't matter to the Brat. All he wanted was to go back to Mummy's shack to get his chest of silver, even though the whole reason the tramp-girl had left it there was so Mummy wouldn't come chasing after her—and *us*—looking for it.

Up front, a far more interesting conversation was taking place. The tramp-girl was telling the Cruel and Goody how she wound up with Mummy.

(I *know* I wasn't there to hear it. But I've listened to the story so many times since, it's as *if* I was there.)

It went like this:

A few weeks after she was born, the tramp-girl's parents died from the Spanish flu and she got sent to live with her grandparents, who then got dead too. After that, she got passed around from aunt to uncle to cousin to ever more distant relatives until she just started getting left with total strangers. Her luck hit rock bottom the day she was dumped with Mummy.

At every stop, she had to work to earn her keep. At first, the jobs were honest: potato farming, fur trapping, cod fishing, pearl diving, chestnut roasting, shoe cobbling, trapeze flying, elephant training—you name it, she did it. And then came the less honest professions: pickpocketing, lockpicking, safecracking, and—with Mummy—stealing, smuggling, and scamming.

Not that she had a choice. "Not if I wanted food or a place to sleep."

Oh, and she always got a new name wherever she went. She had been called Louisa and Marie and Josephine and Luc—"Which isn't even a *girl's* name!"—and a half dozen other ones before Mummy started calling her Pearl.

"I always hated that name," she said.

"Then why did Mummy call you that?"

"*Because* I hated it."

After a couple of hours, we arrived at our destination: a fishing shack on a lake.

"Where's the lake?" the Rude said after we got let out.

The thief-girl pointed down.

"We just drove in on it," she said.

"Really?" the Rude said, looking down. "Aces!"

"Can't M-M-M-Mummy find you here?" the Know-It-All said. "Find *u-u-u-us* here?"

"No," she said. "She doesn't know about this place. It belonged to one of my uncles. He used to take me ice fishing here until one warm spring day when the ice cracked and he fell in. It was too bad. I liked that uncle."

"It's not very safe to be related to you, is it?" the Cruel said.

Inside the hut, it was freezing, so we scavenged for any wood we could find. The Hooligan took an old chair by the back and smashed it against the wall.

"Hey, I wanted to *sit* there!" the Rude said.

"Too late, twerp."

The Cruel pulled up a floorboard and fed that to the potbelly stove, too.

Finally,

WARMTH!

"And f-f-food!"

The Know-It-All had raided the cupboards and found some moldy old cheese that he melted in a pot. The Brat turned up his nose at it, but I wasn't too proud. I stuck a fork in it, pulled out a long, gooey string, and sucked it up.

As we ate, Pearl-not-Pearl told us that if we wanted to get to the coast of Labrador—to the lighthouse—we couldn't take a ship or a train or a car.

"There is only one way this time of year," she said. "Dogsleds."

"Dogsleds!" the Rude said. "I *love* dogs."

"Where are we going to get d-d-dogsleds?" the Know-It-All said.

"And coats," the Hooligan said. "I'm half-frozen to death."

"I have another uncle—Claude—who owns a trading post," she said. "It's not far. We can go first thing in the morning and buy the dogs from him. *And* coats."

"With what money?" the Brat said. "Thanks to you, we don't have any!"

"No, but we have the truck. And the bottles of booze," she said. "Around here, that counts as money."

"And why should we trust you?" the Brat said.

"Because you have no choice. Not if you want to go to Santa's," she said.

"Huddle up, No-Good Ninesters!" I said. The Cruel

rolled her eyes at me, but we all gathered and whispered so Pearl-not-Pearl couldn't hear.

The Brat was not in favor of the new plan, but the rest of us were. For one thing, what choice *did* we have? And for another—DOGSLEDS!

"But if we're gonna do this," I said, "*she* has to be a member."

The Cruel had us take a vote. It came out six to one.

"O.K.," she said to the tramp-girl. "We're in. And so are you."

She smiled.

"But if you're going to join our group," I said, "you need a No-Good Name."

"How about the **THIEF**!" the Brat said, still grumpy that his one vote couldn't overrule everyone else's anymore.

"That's fine by me," she said. "It's as good as any other name I've ever had."

"It's settled, then. You are now officially the **Thief**!" I said. Then I took out my own piece of coal and smudged a big 9 on her forehead. (Nice touch, right?) "Full-fledged member of the No-Good Nine!"

"But aren't we eight?" the Thief said.

"Which is only *one* away from nine!!" I said. "We're almost there!"

One for nine, and nine for one!

◆ ◆ ◆

Meanwhile...

Did you forget about the Vainglorious and my arch-enemy? The two of them had only just arrived in Quebec. About that:

I am beginning to understand why the No-Good Nine wanted to leave Glorious behind.

The entire trip, he has been looking out the window of the train. I thought that he really liked looking at the scenery but now I realize that he only looks at himself in the reflection of the glass.

He is incapable of having a conversation that is not about him and believes he is going to become a movie star.

He is completely delusional. I wonder where and when I can leave him behind.

As we arrive in Quebec City he tells me that the No-Good Nine are going to the Ritz. I fear that I have made a grave mistake trusting him. How could a group of children afford the world-famous Ritz-Carlton?

As we arrive, my fears are confirmed. I am told that no children without an adult are checked in.

But in questioning employees, I talk to a

clerk who says that a group of children did come the night before, but there was no space at the hotel. He says that one of them was very obnoxious.

GLORIOUS: "That had to be the Brat! Oh, he's my BEST friend!"

Further investigation reveals that they had arrived and departed with a girl well known to hotel employees. She lives by the docks, and her mother is some sort of baker. The French they speak here is difficult to comprehend so I am unable to exactly understand who this person is, but the hotel clerk is able to give me her address.

The domicile we arrive at appears to be in poor condition. We know it is the correct house because out front there is a truck marked

MUMMY RUMMY'S
HOME-BAKED YUMMIES

For us, it was just as well we had no idea that my archenemy and the Vainglorious were chasing us, let alone that they had made it to Mummy's. After all, we had enough to worry about as it was. In fact, if we had known what was waiting for us in our next episode, we would never have followed the Thief.

At least, *one* of us wouldn't have.

Because, you see, something *really* bad is going to happen to someone. Something GRUESOME.

If you have the stomach for it, read on! And you'll find out how a member of the No-Good Nine came to look the way he—or *she*—does.

Now maybe stop and use the bathroom, or go get a glass of water. You'll need it!

EPISODE FOUR:
MUSH!

⌁▸▴◂⌁

---

22. OFF TO THE RACES

The Thief parked the truck in front of a rough wooden sign that read

BAWDY CLAUDE'S
TRADING POST

Below, smaller signs read

Siberia→ 3,421 mi
476 mi ←Boondocks
Middle of Nowhere→ 2 mi

"Uncle Claude's idea of a joke," the Thief said, letting us out of the back of the truck.

It didn't seem like much of a joke. Here was as close to nowhere as I'd ever been.

Inside, we found Bawdy Claude himself, all burly, bearded, and bearlike. The only parts of his face not covered by hair were his eyes, nose, and lips.

He and the Thief kissed each other on the cheeks, which was weird. At first they were all friendly, but as they talked, the conversation turned to arguing and swearing. It was all in French, which I was starting to understand. The swear words, anyway. *Tabarnouche* seemed to be the favorite.

They must have settled on a price, because the arguing stopped and they were spitting in their hands and shaking on it.

Following Claude out the back, the Thief explained that she'd traded the truck and booze for two teams of dogs, a pair of sleds, eight fur coats, and a dozen cases of canned food, as well as a few other supplies, like matches. Behind the store, we walked into the kennel to meet our dogs.

"Puppies!" Goody-Two-Shoes said.

"Zese are not *puppies!*" Claude said, his accent as thick as maple syrup. "Zese are *sled* dogs! Zey are professional work animals!"

"They're licking me!" Goody said. She got swallowed up in a huddle of fur and wagging tails.

The only one not petting the dogs was the Hooligan. Every time a dog barked, he jumped like a firecracker had landed at his feet.

"Is the big tough gang member afraid of the little *puppies*?" the Cruel said.

"Haw!" the Rude laughed. The Hooligan slugged him in the shoulder.

Claude harnessed the dogs to the sleds, telling us how to do it as he went.

"I know how to work a dogsled, Claude," the Thief said, taking a seat in one. "*Tabarnouche,* I can beat *you* in a race!"

Claude shot her a dirty look and said the instructions weren't for her, they were for us. When he was done, he asked who wanted to drive the other team.

"Me! Me!" the Brat said.

"No, me!" the Cruel said.

The dogs just sat there.

"What are the two of you, five years old?" Goody-Two-Shoes said. "Take turns!"

The Cruel did not like to be ordered around. She shot Goody-Two-Shoes her frostiest look, but Goody didn't even blink. One thing was for sure—*they* weren't going to be on the same team!

I knew whose team *I* wanted to be on, though, so I quick hopped onto the Thief's sled right up front next to her. Goody-Two-Shoes and the Know-It-All fast climbed in back with the supplies, which meant that the Hooligan and the Rude got stuck in the other sled with the Cruel and the Brat, now arguing over who would lead the team first. While they did, the Thief gave the signal and the dogs started pulling.

"Mush! Mush! Mush!" she cried.

This was *soooo* aces!

"We need to turn slightly to the north-northeast," the Know-It-All called from the back, consulting his compass. "According to my estimation, we will make it to the lighthouse in Black Tickle in 315 hours, which is to say 13.25 days, based on an average speed of 82.5 miles per day."

Did he always have to ruin everything with math?

Our sled glided along gracefully, its runners laying lines in the snow like railroad tracks, while the other sled jerked around in fits and spits, and left a trail that just looked broken.

The Brat and the Cruel were *terrible* at dogsledding.

"You're doing it all wrong!"

"No, *you* are!"

As they argued and flailed, the Thief kept having to stop to let them catch up.

At last, the Cruel got the dogs going forward, and the Thief let them pass us.

From the back of their sled, the Hooligan let out a "Woo-hoo!" while the Rude blew us a raspberry.

"Slowpokes!"

The Thief followed but hung back.

"Don't you want to pass them?" I said.

She smiled. "Not yet."

"It's not a race, you know!" Goody-Two-Shoes called to them.

"Well, let's *make* it a race!" the Hooligan yelled back.

"Yeah!" the Rude hollered.

"Oh, you want a *race*?" the Thief called, pretending to be surprised. "Yes, we can have a race!"

So we did.

But it wasn't even fair. It was like our team was an Olympic sprinter, and their team was some klutzy kid with his shoelaces tied together.

"We've lost sight of them!" Goody said.

The Thief halted the team and we waited for them to catch up.

"Do you want to try again?" she asked smirkily.

"Yes!" the Brat said. "But this time *I* mush!"

But it didn't matter. Our team won again.

And again.

And again.

And

again.

"I think you were a little closer that time!" the Thief called as they approached. "We could almost hear you losing!"

The Brat got off the sled and threw his hat down, having one of his ruby-red tantrums.

"You call that mushing? You have no clue what you're

doing!" the Cruel said, getting off the sled to yell at him. "*I'm* driving this time!"

"Aw, the both a y'uns stink at this!" the Hooligan said. "Let someone else have a try!"

The Rude didn't need to be told twice.

The moment he got in the driver's seat, he was ten times better than either the Cruel or the Brat. The dogs immediately responded to his voice and started pulling straight ahead.

"This is easy!" the Rude said. "It's just like horses!"

"Hey, wait up!" the Brat called, suddenly realizing that he and the Cruel were getting left behind. They had to run as hard as they could to catch up and hop-fall-tumble into the back.

They caught up to our sled, and the race was **ON**!

And this time the winner wasn't a foregone conclusion.

"On MAYHEM, on MONSTER! On THRASHER, on BLITZKRIEG!" the Rude yelled.

I have to admit, I was jealous. Those were *swell* names. (Goody had named ours Buster and Fluffy and Cuddles and Icy-Paws.) The dogs must've liked them too, because they were going faster.

This time, the race lasted a long time. We were neck and neck, our team nudging ahead, then the Rude's, then ours again. But our dogs started to fade, and the Thief quit the race.

"We won!" the Hooligan said, slapping the Rude on the back. "Way to go, twerp!"

"Finally!" the Thief said. "A worthy opponent!"

The Cruel and the Brat just sulked.

The Know-It-All, meanwhile, had no idea a race had even been had. He was too busy measuring the sun with a sextant.

"We should make camp," he said, checking his results against his pocket watch and jotting down numbers in his notebook. "With the declination of the sun, I calculate dusk will come in forty-two minutes."

Instead of making a shelter, however, we tore into the cases of canned food. We were starving! The Rude opened a can of peas and drank them.

The food warmed up our insides, but the problem was the outside. The sun was dropping as fast as a basketball through a hoop, and the temperature plummeted right along with it.

It was *freezing*.

Actually, it was way below freezing.

And then it started to snow.

This was not good.

23. CAMPFIRE TALES

If it hadn't yet occurred to me that the only way *this*—a bunch of idiot kids flinging themselves headlong into the subarctic wilderness in the middle of winter—could end was with all of us freezing to death, it really should've occurred to me now.

Our only hope of making it through the night out here was the Thief. She claimed to have had a half-Inuit second cousin she once lived with who taught her how to survive worse weather than this.

Then she built the snow cave.

"Are you *sure* that's what it's supposed to look like?" I said.

"I think it's pretty good!" the Thief said.

But it really wasn't.

"According to my manuals," the Know-It-All said, "a properly built snow shelter—"

"Aw shuddup!" the Hooligan said. "You and your books! You can't even read a boat schedule!"

"Are you guys *ever* going to stop bringing that up?" the Know-It-All said.

"No!" the Brat, the Rude, and the Hooligan said in unison.

It was really dark now.

And I was really cold.

The kind of cold I had been feeling at the end of last chapter was *nothing* compared to the kind of cold I felt right now.

"I'll make the fire," the Rude said. "Where's the wood?" He looked to the Thief.

"What wood?" she said. "We couldn't bring wood! How would the dogs be able to pull *wood*?"

"So how are we going to make a fire?"

The Thief shook her head. "No fire."

"*NO* fire?"

And **now** it occurred to me that we were a bunch of idiot kids about to freeze to death.

"Fire! Fire! We need *fiiiiiire!*" the Rude said, his teeth chattering.

"Unless you see any chairs or floorboards around," the Cruel said, "tough it out."

"But we *do* have something!" Goody-Two-Shoes said, reaching into her pocket. She had what was in all of our pockets. "Coal!"

Right! The coal Santa had left us! I took my lump out of my pocket, and so did everyone else. It wound up we had all brung it.

Goody passed around a tin can for us to put the coal in, and the Know-It-All lit it.

This was a momentous moment! The burning of the

Christmas coal! Something important had to be said. Something to mark its place forever in time. I opened my mouth and

cough **cough**

almost hacked up a lung. The coal smoke was blowing right in my face.

This stuff was awful!

We all warmed ourselves as best we could without being downwind.

"Hey, quit hoggin' all the heat!" the Hooligan said, trying to push the Rude out of the way.

But the Rude didn't pay any attention.

"Next year, I'm gonna send Santa my Christmas list and I'm only gonna put one thing on it," he said. "**Coal!** That'll really blow the old elf's mind. He'll have to give me something else, or he'll be giving me *exactly* what I ask for."

"Yeah!" the Hooligan said. "Let's *all* do that. We write that we only want coal so's we can stay warm, and beg him please, *please* don't give us no toys! Then he'll leave us some fer sure!"

"I'm sure Santa will fall for that plan," the Cruel said. "Outwitted by Tweedledum and Tweedledummer."

"Well, we'll be playing with Santa's t-t-toys sooner than I had calculated," the Know-It-All said. "We made such good time today, I'm revising my estimate down to only 10.37 days to reach Black Tickle. And once we get to the magical lighthouse, it shouldn't take any t-t-time at all before we are whisked to the North Pole!"

"What's it going to be like?" Goody said. "Santa's workshop."

The Know-It-All got all know-it-all-y, telling us exactly what it was going to be like. How all the elves lived in gingerbread cottages and loved their work, and how Santa was so kind to them and made sure they never worked too hard. "Oh, and the toys!" he went on. "They make every kind of toy in the world. Millions of them!"

The coal was nearly burned out, and it started getting cold again.

"Forget Santa's. We're never gonna make it anywhere if we don't figure out some way to stay warm," the Brat said.

"All we need to keep us warm is right over there," the Thief said. She was pointing toward the dogs, all huddled up in one mass of fur and tails. "Each one is like a warm stove. We either have to sleep on top of them, or each other."

"I'll take one of these mutts over one of *you* any day," the Cruel said, getting up.

Me, I was used to sleeping between a bunch of sweaty, smelly brothers and sisters, so it was downright nice to cozy up between a couple of fuzzy dogs. And they *were* warm!

Finally, we were on our way! It felt pretty swell.

Of course, we would have felt a lot less swell if we had known what had been happening back in a certain rickety shack in Quebec.

◆ ◆ ◆

Meanwhile . . .

If you remember, we last left the Truant Officer and the Vainglorious as they arrived at the shack of Mummy Rummy.

I get a heart attack just *thinking* about that place!

So I'll let my archenemy tell you what happened:

> We knock on the front door and are met by a woman who identifies herself as Mummy Rummy.
>
> Mrs. Rummy seems unhappy to be disturbed.
>
> When I say why we are here, however, she becomes interested. Then distressed.
>
> It happens that her own daughter, Pearl, is now a runaway. The child brought the No-Good Nine to her house yesterday and Mrs. Rummy gave them food and shelter. This morning, Mrs. Rummy helped the American children in their travels by driving them outside of the city, only to return home to discover that her own daughter was gone. She

fears that Pearl has gone off to join them.

Mrs. Rummy begins crying at the thought that the children are all alone in the snowy wilderness.

Mummy was pretty good at that fake crying thing—at faking out everyone.

The real story was that Mummy had come home from leaving us for dead to find that the Thief had escaped and stolen one of her trucks, as well as something *else*. (I'd tell you what it was, but that would ruin a surprise.) Mummy was boiling mad, and she and the Brothers Jack were just about to go in search of her when my nemesis and the Vainglorious showed up at her door.

It *had* occurred to Mummy that maybe Pearl had gone to find us, but she didn't know exactly where we were going. The Vainglorious, however, said *he* did.

"To the lighthouse at . . . DARK HUMOR!" he said. "On the coast of . . . GOLDEN RETRIEVER!"

Mummy wondered if both the Vainglorious *and* the Truant Officer weren't total morons. She decided to take them along to hunt for us anyway, but she'd never let either of them realize the truth: She wanted the Thief back for one reason and one reason only. To teach that ungrateful wretch a lesson!

From my archenemy's diary, it's pretty clear the big

dope fell for Mummy's good-mother act hook, line, and sinker. What a chump!

(Yeah, I *know* we fell for it, too. But we were just a bunch of stupid kids and he was a former Russian secret agent.)

As for what the Vainglorious thought of Mummy, I have no idea. Other than that he probably wasn't thinking at all.

24. WE WERE NOT ALONE

This dog feels soooo *warm and cozy,* I thought as I slowly began to wake up. *I just have to give it a hug!*

The mutt sure did smell *bad* though—even for a dog.

I opened my eyes. I wasn't hugging a dog.

I was hugging the Rude.

"*Gross!*" I said, pushing him away. "Get off of me!"

And that's when I heard it. People talking outside, in a language I didn't understand.

And it *wasn't* French.

I peeked out of the snow shelter and saw two hooded figures. One short, one tall. The one had a long spear and the other a rifle.

Then I realized—these were Inuit! How far north *were* we?

As quietly as I could, I woke up the others and we crept out of the shelter.

Then *they* saw *us*.

The short one pointed his spear in our direction and said something to the tall one.

"Hey, watch who you're pointin' that stick at!" the Hooligan said, threatening him.

The tall one now took his rifle off his shoulder and started yelling at the Hooligan.

"Oh, yeah?" the Hooligan said, like he could understand what the man was saying. "I'll take on the both a y'uns!"

"Will you stop!" the Thief yelled at the Hooligan. "They aren't going to hurt you, you *tabarnouche*!"

She turned to the hooded figures and talked to them. In *their* language.

"You speak Inuit," the Rude said.

"It's called Inuktitut," the Thief said. "My second cousin, remember?"

It wound up that the two Inuit were a boy our age and his father. They were traveling home and had happened upon our campsite. They were more shocked to find us than we were to see them.

"After all, we don't see many Americans out here," the boy said.

"You speak *English*?" the Rude said.

"Yes," the boy said. "I learn it in school."

The boy's name was Lumiuk and while we were talking his father pointed over to our snow cave and said something.

"Father is asking, *What is that heap of snow?*"

"It's our snow shelter," the Thief said proudly.

"*Shelter?* Father says. *That's the worst shelter I've ever seen!* I'm sorry, but Father can be so rude," Lumiuk said. "He also says that you would have died if it hadn't been so warm last night."

"Warm?" the Rude said. "Last night was *warm?*"

"Oh, yes. It was like an early spring!" Lumiuk said.

His father was now asking another question.

"*Why are you all here?*"

The Know-It-All explained, and Lumiuk's father nodded along like it was all normal. Not because it was in any way normal, but because the people from the south were always talking crazy stuff. As for Lumiuk, he thought it was grand.

"Santa! Oh, I have heard much about him. I would love to travel to his workshop. But then I would love to travel anywhere. Especially the great cities I have read about in books and seen in films."

As it happened, Lumiuk and his dad were headed in the same direction *we* were going.

"Can we *please* travel together?" Lumiuk said. "It is so lonely with just Father."

We huddled to discuss our options.

"What options?" the Rude said. "We're going to all *die* if we don't go with them. If last night was warm, how are we gonna survive one that's normal?"

It was a one-for-nine, nine-for-one moment. But the bigger issue, it wound up, was convincing Lumiuk's father to *let* us come with them.

Lumiuk was definitely trying. In fact, according to the Thief, he was begging.

"He's saying, *We must let them come with us*," the Thief said. "*They will die if we don't help them.* But his dad doesn't seem to care."

In fact, he was completely disgusted by our presence, and wanted no part of us being anywhere near him.

He was a real charmer.

I was hungry and ready for breakfast, so I went and found of can of Del Monte pineapple slices and got out the opener. Lumiuk's father was still shaking his head no, but as soon as I dug into the can and the opener started going

tup tup tup

he stopped and looked at me, and then at the can of food.

He said something. He didn't sound angry anymore.

"Father says you can come with us if you share your food," Lumiuk said. "He loves canned food. In fact, he loves any food."

We all looked at each other.

"Give him the can!" the Brat said, pushing me toward him.

"But I just opened it!" I said.

The Cruel snatched it out of my hand and gave it to Lumiuk's dad, who ate it up so fast it was already gone.

We were in.

25. LIFE WITH THE INUIT

Besides sharing our food, the one thing Lumiuk's father insisted on was that we help do everything that Inuit children were expected to do—hunt, build igloos, and take care of the dogs. It sounded swell!

Unfortunately, it turned out to be far from swell. For one thing, hunting was boring. I had never been hunting before, and while it sounded exciting, it, in fact, was not. It mostly involved a lot of standing around doing nothing.

Well, first it involved a lot of mushing and *then* a lot of standing around doing nothing.

For another thing, Lumiuk's father was a big fat jerk.

It was really disappointing. I had this idea that the Inuit were different from us ever since I was little and saw *Nanook of the North*. It was the supposedly real story of an Inuit hunter—Nanook—who was really nice to his kids and could build an igloo in a flash and instead of kissing his wife, they'd rub noses. He was super-quick with his spear and hunted whatever he wanted, no problem. Which made me wonder why it was taking Lumiuk's father so long to kill *anything*. And why was he using a rifle?

"Spears?" Lumiuk says. "Oh, no, Father would never use one of these old-fashioned things. Guns are much better for killing animals. The spear belonged to my grandfather."

Lumiuk didn't much like hunting, either. Because of this, he was a major disappointment to his father, who was constantly yelling at him and making mean comments. Not that he was only mean to his son. He was mean to all of us.

All day long, Lumiuk's dad told us what we were doing wrong, be it mushing, hunting, or even how we were eating.

Frankly, it wasn't all that different from how my own father treated me, but that was what was so disappointing! In the movie, all the Inuit parents seemed so nice. But I guess parents are the same kind of horrible no matter where you go.

Hunting only got interesting at the end of that day, when we finally came across an animal. Lumiuk's dad held up a finger to

Shhhh!

us.

The animal was some crazy-looking big buffalo thing. "What the heck *is* that?" I whispered.

"A caribou," the Know-It-All whispered back. "Very common to this area, and a typical hunting target across Canada."

"That could feed everyone back home for a week!" Lumiuk whispered, then covered his eyes because he couldn't bear to watch. His father smacked him in the head and motioned for him to look.

Then, Lumiuk's dad moved in for the kill, creeping along the top of the snow as quietly as he could. Slowly— steadily—carefully, he raised his gun.

As exciting as it was, I started to feel bad for the animal, and then I . . . I . . . ah . . . ah . . .

"Ah-*tchoo!*"

"*Gesundheit!*" Goody-Two-Shoes said.

The caribou bolted away.

Lumiuk's father began ranting and raving.

Lumiuk said it wasn't really worth translating.

It was so late by the time Lumiuk's dad calmed down that he decided to make camp right there. No arguments from me! I felt twice as exhausted and frozen as I had yesterday.

Unfortunately, there was no time to rest. The igloo had to be built.

No time to rest for *us*, anyway. Lumiuk's dad relaxed on a sled nestled in his furs and ate tinned food.

Lumiuk might not have been much of a hunter, but he was very good at making igloos. He taught us how to do it, and it was actually kind of fun, cold and hungry though we were.

When the igloo was done, we all felt pretty proud of ourselves. It looked a *lot* better than the Thief's heap of snow.

But there was *still* no time for rest, because Lumiuk's father barked at us to go gather moss to get the fire started. He then

tup tup tup

opened a can of string beans to eat.

While he did, he complained about how he did all the work, and Lumiuk did nothing. *Nothing!*

"The only thing Father considers work is hunting," Lumiuk explained.

Finally, it was time for us to sit around the fire and eat something too.

We got excited when—after having finished his second can of Franco-American spaghetti—Lumiuk's father pulled out slabs of dried seal meat from his sled.

The meat, unfortunately, was not for us.

"That's no fair!" the Brat said as Lumiuk's dad downed chunk after chunk of dried seal. "He's been eating *all* of our canned food. Why don't we get any of his meat?"

"Father says that hunters need to eat food in order to

get food," Lumiuk said. "So only hunters should eat the meat."

But then he started tossing hunks of dried seal to the dogs!

"Without the dogs pulling us, we could never survive," Lumiuk said. "So Father says it is more important to feed the dogs than ourselves."

"But he *is* feeding himself," the Hooligan said.

"Yes. Father hates to be hungry."

We complained so much that Lumiuk's father finally gave us some dried seal to eat.

"But don't eat too much!"

That wasn't going to be a problem. Seal jerky is even worse than it sounds. It was like chewing on an old shoe.

There was nothing to do but go to sleep, except I couldn't even do that, because Lumiuk wouldn't stop talking. He wanted to know everything about what life was like in Pittsburgh and kept saying how much he wanted to visit. "It sounds wonderful!"

"Yeah, wonderful," I said. I then buried my face under a dog and went to sleep.

◆ ◆ ◆

Meanwhile . . .

While we were mushing, Mummy and the two Jacks were dragging my nemesis and the Vainglorious every which way across the frozen countryside. They were searching all the remote hideouts she used for her bootlegging operation, with her telling the Truant Officer they were her "hunting cabins."

Mrs. Mummy certainly is an avid outdoorswoman.

Her two sons, Rooster Jack and Black Jack, speak no English. Even so, Glorious manages to annoy them, perhaps because he doesn't believe that they don't understand him and so keeps talking to them.

Although we as yet have had no luck locating the children, I enjoy driving in this snowy wilderness. It reminds me so much of Mother Russia.

We arrive at our next destination and last hope: Bawdy Claude's Trading Post.

I question Mr. Claude, who promises that he has not seen Pearl, let alone seven American children.

Frustratingly, we appear to have hit a dead end. We walk outside, and Mrs. Mummy goes around back to use the outhouse.

We wait for her. She takes a long time.

Amazingly, when she finally returns, it is having discovered that the children have *taken off on two dogsleds and are headed for the lighthouse of Black Tickle on the coast of Labrador. How she discovered this information in the outhouse, I am not sure.*

Well, *I* know how she figured it out. She went to the outhouse—which is to say the toilet—and saw her stolen van sitting in back of the trading post. Someone had painted graffiti over her sign, so it now read

MUMMY SCUMMY AND HER TWO SONS ARE DUMMIES!

Which was pretty funny. The crazy thing, though, is that I had no idea who did it! One of *us*, I was guessing, but who?

Anyway, Mummy was pretty ticked off at the whole situation, and she went back inside to confront Bawdy Claude.

While I don't know *exactly* what she did to get Claude to rat us out, I'm guessing it involved threats and weaponry.

Not that it mattered. What mattered was that she found out where we were going and that we were mushing our way there. Unfortunately for us, Mummy knew a thing or two about mushing herself.

26. A CHAPTER YOU MIGHT WANT TO SKIP IF YOU'RE SQUEAMISH

I'd tell you what happened on the second day of traveling with the Inuit, except it wasn't that much different from what happened the first day.

Or the third day.

Or any of the days we spent with them.

"We're wasting too much time!" the Know-It-All said. "If it wasn't for all this hunting, we'd already be at the l-l-lighthouse!"

For once, everybody agreed with him. We now knew how to build an igloo lickety-split and get a roaring fire going, so we could survive just fine without Lumiuk and his dad. If not better! Lumiuk's father had practically polished off all our food.

"We're gonna starve if we spend any more time with that guy!" the Hooligan said.

The next morning, we told Lumiuk that we were going off on our own.

He was devastated.

"Why do you have to *go*?" he said, and begged us to stay just a little while longer.

That's when I got the idea.

Snap!

(That was me snapping my fingers.)

"Why don't you *come* with us!" I said. "We could always use another member."

Especially since that would make us *nine*.

Lumiuk was tempted, but he couldn't bear the thought of not seeing his mom or his sisters and the other members of his family again.

"Besides, I'm not naughty like the rest of you."

Being a horrible human being should never be a qualification for joining a club. But in our case, it kinda was.

Before he left, Lumiuk gave me his spear.

"I can't take this," I said. "It was your grandfather's!"

"He wouldn't mind," Lumiuk said. "Grandfather is a lot nicer than father. Besides, you might need it. I've never even used it."

◆ ◆ ◆

For the next few days, we mushed along at our fastest clip yet.

"According to my calculations, we only have 27.88 hours of mushing left before we reach the lighthouse at B-B-Black Tickle!" the Know-It-All said.

We had one tiny little problem, though. We were down to our last can of food. And it was a bad one.

Campbell's Ox Tail Soup.

I opened it, pried out the round frozen brick of meat

stew, and smashed it into pieces. As we each gnawed on a chunk, we discussed what we had to do.

Hunt.

While we had learned certain survival skills, none of us had ever caught an animal.

We *did* have the spear, and even if it wasn't as good as a gun, it was still how people had hunted for thousands of years. It was just a question of getting close enough to an animal to stab it. But we had to *find* one first, and that was no easy thing.

The next day, we mushed along on empty stomachs. We only had two more days of sledding to get to the lighthouse, but there was no way we'd make it without real food.

For lunch, we ate snow.

"We could always eat one of the dogs," the Cruel said.

"We are *not* eating a puppy!" Goody-Two-Shoes said.

"Yeah!" I said. But I couldn't help but wonder what one would taste like. THAT is how hungry I was!

It was after our snow lunch that we had a stroke of luck.

"Hey, what's that?" the Rude said, halting his sled and pointing to a spot over near the coast.

I had no idea how he could see that far, but as we got closer, we saw the spot was a walrus. A *sick* walrus. Even when we got to be standing just a few yards away from it, the animal still wasn't moving.

"Poor walrus," the Rude said, kneeling down. "Sorry we gotta kill ya and eat ya, big feller."

I handed the spear to the Know-It-All.

"What are you h-h-h-handing me *this* for?"

"To kill the walrus," I said.

"Why don't *you* d-d-d-do it!" the Know-It-All said, trying to force it back to me. "You're the one Lumiuk gave the spear to!"

"I can't," I said. "It's against my religion."

"No it's not. You're *C-C-Catholic*."

"But it's a Friday," I said. "And anyway, it'll be a piece of cake. The walrus looks half-dead as it is. You'll just be putting it out of its misery."

"There's no way *I*'m killing it. H-h-here," he said, and handed the spear to the Hooligan.

"Forget it!" the Hooligan said. "If it was the Brat y'uns wanted me to spear, I'd do it. But I ain't spearin' no walrus!"

He handed the spear to the Rude, who also refused.

"Each of those tusks is bigger than my whole body!" he said. "Besides, I *found* it. I already did my job!"

The only boy left was the Brat.

"Fine!" the Brat said, taking the weapon. "I *will* do it."

The Brat took a few steps toward the walrus, the snow crunching under his feet. He stopped and poised the spear right by his ear, ready to lunge. Then the walrus turned and looked up at him.

It had the face of an old dog.

Pleading.

Sweet.

Loving.

The Brat froze. And stayed frozen.

He couldn't do it.

"*Tsk tsk tsk,*" the Cruel went. "I'm disappointed in you."

With a sneer, she snatched the spear out of his hand. Then she turned to the Thief.

"And you?" the Cruel said, offering her the weapon. "Boys are all weak when you get right down to it, but *you*? Don't you have a great-uncle once removed who taught you how to use a spear? Or are you like the boys? Nothing but *talk*."

The Thief looked down at her feet.

"But the walrus is just so *cute*. . . ."

The Cruel turned to Goody-Two-Shoes and offered the spear to her.

Goody was defiant.

"I would never kill *any*thing," she said. "Killing is wrong."

"Oh yeah? What about all that seal jerky you've been eating?" the Cruel said. "Those seals didn't have mothers?"

Goody looked at her with burning eyes. Boy, did she *not* like the Cruel.

The Cruel now turned to the walrus, still looking up

with those puppy-dog eyes. The Cruel flashed her wicked smirk.

I didn't doubt for a minute that she'd do it—that she'd kill that sweet, beautiful, innocent animal. I admired her for it. And was disgusted by her, too.

Brimming with confidence, the Cruel stepped into striking distance. Then she raised the spear, took aim, and

LUNGED

for the walrus's heart!

At the moment the point of the spear stuck flesh, the walrus came alive.

The massive animal reared up, with the weapon stuck in its chest and the Cruel still holding on. Just as fast, the beast came back down, the spear splintering under its weight. The Cruel fell in a heap on top of the broken weapon and scrambled to get up, but the walrus got up faster. Whether in self-defense or to attack or just trying to get out of the way, the walrus thrust a tusk at the Cruel. It wasn't as sharp as the spear, but it did the same kind of damage.

Except instead of piercing the Cruel in the chest, it went right through her left eye.

That's right. Her *eye*.

It went

POP!

The walrus pulled away from her, and the Cruel was unconscious before she hit the hard, icy snow.

Blood was gushing from where her eye used to be.

Now do you see why I said you might not want to read this?

27. AND YOU MIGHT WANT TO SKIP THIS PART TOO

Blood.

It looked so much more red against the white of the snow. But only for a moment. It quickly burned down through the white powder, causing steam to rise up.

It was like I couldn't even move—like my body was locked up. In terror.

Terror at what had happened to the Cruel. And the walrus.

Blood was spilling out of the animal, from where the point of the spear was lodged in its chest.

The walrus

ROARED

at us.

It did not seem happy.

Slowly, it made its way—right flipper, left flipper—to the edge of the ice, but before it could dive into the water, it collapsed. And died.

As for the Cruel, it was an ugly situation. What was left of her left eye was—

Well, maybe it's better *not* to describe it.

Obviously, the right thing to do was to run and help her. But I couldn't. I was still just stuck there. All of us were.

Except Goody-Two-Shoes.

She went to the Cruel and held her head in her arms, wiping the blood away from her face with her sleeve.

"I-i-i-is she . . ." the Know-It-All said. "Dead?"

"No," Goody-Two-Shoes said. "She's passed out. But we have to stop the bleeding."

Goody-Two-Shoes packed snow onto the Cruel's eye to ice it down.

Then, she went to her bag and fetched out her sewing kit.

Remember when we first met Goody, and her mom mentioned that she volunteered at the hospital? Well, that was about to come in real handy.

At the hospital, she had watched doctors stitch up lots of cuts. She had never done it herself, but she knew how it was done. And she had sewn up plenty of things before.

Just never something alive.

Goody threaded the needle in one go, her hands as steady as the ground. How she could be so calm? *I* was shaking all over, and I wasn't even doing anything!

"Whattya gonna do with that needle?" the Hooligan said.

"You're not g-g-going to . . ." the Know-It-All said.

"Are you *really* . . . ?" the Brat said.

"She needs stitches," Goody said. "It's the only way to stop the bleeding."

"I have to close my eyes," the Hooligan said.

"Forget that!" the Rude said. "This is jake!"

It only took one pass of the needle through the eyelids, however, for the Rude to cover his eyes, too.

Stitch by stitch, Goody-Two-Shoes threaded the lids together.

I was impressed. How could you *not* be?

After she finished, the left side of the Cruel's face was a gory mess. The eye was purple and black and looked like it was swollen shut.

"I don't care whether or not you *are* a goody-two-shoes," the Hooligan said, finally opening his eyes. "You're the toughest kid I ever met!"

I took off my jacket and so did the Rude. We made a bed for the Cruel in the sled, and the Hooligan and the Brat lifted her onto it.

Mayhem—one of the dogs on her team—came up and sniffed the sleeping Cruel, then licked her hand.

"What do we do n-n-n-now?" the Know-It-All asked.

"What else?" the Rude said. "We eat!"

"But *how*?" the Brat said. "Does anyone know how to turn a dead walrus into steak?"

We all stared at the big lump lying on the edge of the ice.

The Thief took out her shiny knife.

"I had a great-aunt twice removed who was married to a butcher."

Now I *could* tell you what happened next, but I figure I've already put you through enough. Besides, a kid losing an eye is one thing. But cutting up a poor old walrus and eating it? That's downright disturbing!

◆ ◆ ◆

We were all sitting around the fire, appreciating that for once we had full bellies. The Rude was telling some story about the boxing gym—or maybe it was the racetrack—while I drew pictures in the snow with the broken-off end of the spear I had pulled out of the walrus.

"I want to see a mirror."

The voice came from behind me. It was *her*.

The Cruel was conscious again.

"I said I want to see a mirror," she said. "**Now!**"

The only thing we had that you could see yourself in was the Thief's knife, so she handed it to her.

The Cruel looked into the blade, tilting it at different angles so she could see herself.

"Who sewed my eye shut?" she said, still looking at herself.

We all pointed to Goody-Two-Shoes.

I assumed she was going to say something mean—since that's what she always did—but instead the Cruel spoke words I *never* thought would pass her lips:

"Thank you."

Goody accepted it with a nod and a smile.

"Hey, did the Cruel just say the *T* word?" the Rude said. "How much blood did she *lose*?"

The Brat slapped him up the side of the head.

"How do you f-f-f-feel?" the Know-It-All asked.

"I feel fine," she said. "It's just an eye."

Just an eye?

"O.K., maybe *you're* the toughest kid I ever met," the Hooligan said.

"We made this for you," the Thief said.

It was an eyepatch, cut out of a piece of black leather with a strap attached.

The Cruel put it on.

It looked *swell*!

"Wow," the Rude said. "You look like a pirate!"

"And you look like a turtle that lost its shell."

The Cruel smirked.

And now you know how the Cruel got her eyepatch, in case you've been staring at the front cover this whole time and wondering.

28. HELLO, LIGHTHOUSE!

"By my calculations of last night's stars plus the position of Venus in regard to the sun, I am fairly certain that we are within three and a half *m-m-m-miles* of the lighthouse!"

"WUDJA SAY?!" the Rude screamed.

The Know-It-All was sitting backward on the sled, facing the team the Rude was driving.

The Know-It-All repeated what he said, as loud as he could.

"WUZZAT MEAN?" the Rude yelled, pulling closer.

"We're almost there!" the Know-It-All shouted.

"WHY DINTCHA JUST SAY SO?" the Rude hollered, pulling past us and into the lead.

We were all excited to be so close. "Hey, Know-It-All," I said. "Why don't you read that article again?"

In the last few hours, the Know-It-All must've read the story ten times, but I wanted to hear it once more.

I loved when he got to the part that goes:

> "It is always warm in Santaland, even though it is located at the North Pole. But what else would

you expect from the most magical place on earth?

"As for the elves, they whistle as they skip their way home from work. And why not? They have the most fulfilling job there is—making toys for children—and just might live in the most beautiful workers' housing ever constructed. Their gingerbread cottages stand just—"

"So they can actually *eat* their houses?" I said. "Wouldn't they just fall down?"

"No," the Know-It-All said. "Gingerbread cottages aren't made *of* gingerbread, they're just decorated to look like it. It's the V-V-V-Victorian style."

The Know-It-All kept reading, getting to the part about the factory and how the elves were able to make so many toys.

"Do you think they have bikes?" the Thief asked.

"Of course they have b-b-bicycles!" the Know-It-All said. "If it can be a Christmas present, they make it!"

Up ahead, the Rude suddenly halted his sled.

"Hey, why are you stopping?" the Thief said, pulling our sled up alongside his.

"There it **is**!" the Rude said.

He was pointing off in the distance. It took a minute, but then I saw it too. The lighthouse! It was hard to make out, being all white against the bright sky, but it looked like some kind of fairy-tale tower rising out of the snowy plain. The light at the top swiveled toward us, flashing once like a giant wink, then swung back the other way.

"It even *looks* magical!" Goody-Two-Shoes said.

"Yes!" the Thief said. "It has to be!"

"We made it!" the Hooligan said, taking off his cap and putting it over his heart. A sob was choking his throat. "We really *made* it!"

"Well?" the Brat said. "What are you two *waiting* for?"

The drivers looked at each other and

"Mush! Mush! **Mush!**" the Thief yelled.

"On VAMPIRE, on VIRUS! On KILLER, on DE-MON!" the Rude hollered.

The dogs were running faster than ever, like even *they* were excited to get there!

As we neared the base of the lighthouse, we had to crane our necks to still find the light, the top of it was so tall.

We pulled up to the bright red front door of the lighthouse.

"What do we do now?" I said, getting out of the sled.

"We go in!" the Brat said.

"Should we knock?" Goody said.

But we didn't have to.

The red door opened all by itself.

Well, not *all* by itself. There was a lumbering old

man pushing it open from the inside, with a crinkly old woman right behind him.

They looked mighty surprised to see us.

"WHO THE HELL ARE *YE* ALL!?!"

And not that happy, either.

29. NOT 100 PERCENT WHAT WE WERE EXPECTING

"What're ye *eight* children doin' here?" the lighthouse keeper said. "And with *dogsleds*, no less! Are ye Inuit, or aliens?"

"We're neither," the Brat said. "We're Americans."

"**Americans!**" Mr. Keeper hollered. "Why on earth are ye in Black Tickle?"

"We're here to signal the n-n-narwhal," the Know-It-All said.

"Nar-*what*?" Mrs. Keeper said, as dumbfounded as her husband.

"The magic narwhal," the Know-It-All said. "The one who answers the Morse code signal from the l-l-lamp and pulls the golden barge that takes visitors to Santa's. It's all right here in this article. You both are in it t-t-t-too!" He handed his written-out copy to the keepers.

Mr. and Mrs. Keeper stood reading it, their lips moving as their eyes crawled left to right and back again. They were stupefied.

"He believed it!" Mr. Keeper said. "That fool actually done *believed* it!"

"Believed *what?*" the Cruel said.

"That balderdash I told him!" Mr. Keeper said. "That reporter was another one of those southerners tryin' to stir up trouble for us folk up north. Tryin' to stir up trouble for Santy! So I made up a whole bunch of nonsense about how me lighthouse is magic and how I could signal Santy. And he done printed it! And ye foolish children *believed* it! Ye are more the fools than him!"

We must've all looked pretty upset, because Mrs. Keeper kicked the back of her husband's leg and said, "Don't be makin' fun of them, ye horrid man!" She turned to us. "Ye poor children, ye come all this way and for nudd'n! Just looks at the sad eyes on all ye faces!"

"Wait a *minute*," the Cruel said. "Are you saying that there are *no* magic narwhals? And there is *no* way to signal Santa? Or to get to his workshop from here?"

Mr. and Mrs. Keeper both shrugged and shook their heads.

We were stunned.

"You dragged us all the way up here for **nothing**!" the

Cruel said, turning to the Know-It-All. "You aren't the *Know*-It-All—you're the Know-*Nothing*-at-All!"

"She's right!" the Hooligan said.

The Know-It-All got that vomitty look of his. Then he buried his face in his hands.

"You're *right*!" the Know-It-All said. "I *am* a know-nothing! Magic *narwhals!* A *g-g-golden* barge! How could I have ever believed it!? I'm such an idiot, and it's all my *fault!*"

"You are *not* an idiot!" Goody-Two-Shoes said to him. Then she turned to the rest of us. "Don't blame him! We all heard the story before we decided to come, and we *all* had the chance to turn back plenty of times!"

"Goody is right," the Thief said. "And think of what we've done. We traveled a thousand miles by dogsled in the middle of winter!"

"The dogsleds *are* swell," the Rude said.

"It sure beats hangin' around the Mug Uglies," the Hooligan said.

"Or boarding school," the Brat said.

"Or my family," I said, because I couldn't think of anything else to say.

"Or the orphanage."

Everyone looked at the Cruel.

"Did you just say something . . ." Goody said. "*Positive?*"

The Cruel then did something even *more* strange. She smiled. Not an icy-sarcastic-hateful smirk, but a *smile*.

"I guess we're *all* a bunch of know-nothing-at-alls," she said.

"*No-Good* know-nothin'-at-alls," the Rude said.

"The No-Good Know-Nothin' Nine!" I said, and flashed the Sign of the Nine across my chest. "Nine for one, and one for nine!"

"What does that even *mean*?" the Cruel said.

"Come on, ye children," Mrs. Keeper said. "Come inside where it's warm and I'll start makin' ye a fine fish stew!"

"When ye taste her cookin' ye'll *really* regret comin' to Black Tickle!" Mr. Keeper said.

"I said shuddup, ye horrid man!"

"Come with me first," the keeper said to us. "I'll show ye how to work the beacon."

"You mean the light? The lighthouse light?" the Rude said. "Now *that's* swell!"

"Me **first**!" the Brat said, pushing his way up ahead.

"I w-w-w-want to go first!" the Know-It-All said. "It's a Chance 55 mm!"

Their voices echoed off the stone walls of the lighthouse as we climbed up the spiral staircase, with me last. Well, next to last. Goody-Two-Shoes was behind me. But where *was* she?

I looked back and didn't see her.

But I did hear the sobbing.

◆ ◆ ◆

Goody was sitting on the step outside, bawling her eyes out.

"I didn't want anyone to see me cry," she said to me when I came back out. But now that she'd started, she couldn't stop.

"What's wrong?" I said.

"It's just all we've *been* through!" she said when she was finally able to speak. "First, we almost got arrested by the Truant Officer and killed by Mummy, and if it hadn't been for Lumiuk and his father we would've died for sure, and then the Cruel lost her *eye* and the walrus died and we *ate* it and now there's no way to get to Santa's but I don't *want* to go home because when I do I'm going to wish I *were* in jail or killed or dead or had only lost an eye because my parents will be so horrible to me!"

She started to bawl again, so I put my arm around her. I didn't know what to say. I could've said none of it was a big deal, but for once lying didn't seem like the right thing to do.

Goody took out a handkerchief to blow her nose, and said, "I just never wanted anything in my life so badly as to go to Santa's."

"I think I can help you, me ducky."

We turned and saw Mrs. Keeper. She had heard everything.

"I can't stand to watch a poor child cry," she said, and wiped a tear away from Goody.

"I shouldn't be tellin' this to ye, me children. Not to *any* southerner," Mrs. Keeper said. "But we weren't being totally honest with ye kiddies. There's *more* to the story."

"What story?" Goody said. "What weren't you being honest about?"

"About not knowin' how to get to Santa's."

◆ ◆ ◆

Meanwhile...

You don't think my archenemy and Mummy just gave up, do you? Because they didn't.

Mummy was so good at mushing that she and her crew should have beaten us to the lighthouse, especially considering how much time we wasted with the Inuit. *Should* have, but didn't, because she wasn't nearly so good with a compass as she was with a dog whip.

Instead of taking a diagonal path across the snowy interior like we had, she headed straight to the coast and then turned north. A couple of times Mummy thought she had caught our trail, only to find out the sled tracks were from Inuit hunters.

Meanwhile, my nemesis kept at his journal.

I will be happy for one thing when this is over: never again having to listen to this child!

Glorious does nothing but complain about how cold he is all the time. I tell him that this is summer compared to Siberia, but he is just another weak American child.

Mummy and her two sons, on the other hand, are not weak at all. They know how to mush the dogs, although I can't say they treat them well.

We have been traveling north along the coast for days when Mummy suddenly stops the sled. I ask her why, and she points to the dogs sniffing. She releases them from the harness and they race to a spot near the sea.

When we get there, the snow is red from blood. Lying on the ice is the carcass of some sort of large animal.

Mrs. Mummy goes to the body and sticks her hand inside its rib cage.

"It's still warm," she says.

Uh-oh.

PART TWO

PART TWO

Adventures in Santaland

Have you ever seen our first film, *The No-Good Nine Meets Zorro*? If you did, I'm sorry, and no you can't have your money back.

But do you remember the part where the bad guys figure out Zorro's secret identity and they go to his hacienda and discover us hiding in the stables and there's this great big shoot-out? (Yeah, I *know* it looked fake, but it's a movie!)

Anyway, it was kind of like that when the Truant Officer, the Vainglorious, Mummy, and the two Jacks arrived at Black Tickle. Only with a lot more snow.

They had been mushing full-speed ever since they found the walrus carcass, and knocked on the lighthouse door just a day after *we* arrived.

Mr. and Mrs. Keeper, god bless 'em, told them that they hadn't seen any kids, and shut the door right in their noses.

I wish I could've seen the look on my nemesis's face! He must've been totally crushed.

Mummy, unfortunately, knew they were lying. In fact, she was sure we were there.

I ask why she is so positive, and Mrs. Mummy points to footprints in the snow. They are of different shapes and sizes, and they are fresh.

A clue I should not have missed!

We explore the area surrounding the lighthouse, which sits on a cliff overlooking the sea. Noises are coming from an outbuilding. Someone—or some children!—are inside.

Quietly we approach the building. After a silent count of three, I thrust open the door to discover . . .

DOGS!

These must be the sled dogs of the American children. The No-Good Nine were here—and maybe still are!

A further search of the premises, however, turns up no evidence of them.

Until, that is, we find a message painted on the cliff overlooking the dock.

WE KAME. WE SAW. WE KROSST THE LINE.

NOW IT'S AU REVOIR
TO THE NO-GOOD NINE!

I had no idea *which* of us was writing the graffiti, but it sure was a swell goodbye note.

We might've left, but Mummy was determined to find out where we had gone.

As to how she would get this bit of information, she told my archenemy that she would go have a talk with Mrs. Keeper.

"Mother to mother."

When she confronted her, Mrs. Keeper refused to say where we had gone. Until Mummy did something *really* wicked.

Do you want to know how bad—how truly *evil*—Mummy was?

She threatened to shoot the dogs.

All of them!

Miraculously, Mrs. Mummy's mother-to-mother appeal worked.

MUMMY: "I just begged 'er to 'ave mercy on a poor parent. I threw myself on my knees in tears and kind Mrs. Keeper took pity on me and told me where the children 'ad gone."

As it turns out, the No-Good Nine left on a mail boat, bound for a mysterious place called Isle X.

Before we get to what we were doing on that ship, however, let's go back to the night before, when me and Goody-Two-Shoes were sitting on the front step of the lighthouse. Because I was just dying to know: What wasn't Mrs. Keeper being honest about?

EPISODE FIVE:
ISLE X

30. THE GREAT AND AMAZING ADVENTURE

When she said there was more to the story, Mrs. Keeper wasn't kidding.

(Of course, if there *hadn't* been more to the story, this would've been an awfully short book.)

"I shouldn't be tellin' ye this," Mrs. Keeper said. "I *really* shouldn't!"

But she did.

"Santy don't live at the North Pole—that's just a way of throwin' ye outsider folk off," Mrs. Keeper said. "All the people of the north know he and his worker elves are situated on an island up in Baffin Bay—an island that don't appear on any map." She leaned in and whispered its name:

"Isle X."

Isle X. What a *swell* name!

"Can you really get there by magic narwhal?" Goody-Two-Shoes asked.

"Ye can get there, but it don't have nudd'n' to do with narwhals," Mrs. Keeper said. "There's a boat."

The boat, it wound up, was a steamer that ran a course up and down the coast of Labrador, bringing supplies and mail to the lighthouses, including Black Tickle.

"And when it's done, it makes one final, *secret* stop."

Mrs. Keeper said that she might be able to convince the captain of the boat to take us to the island. "But that don't mean ye should *want* to go. Things are not the same up at the workshop as when I was your age. Ye hear *stories* . . ."

"What stories?" we asked, but she just shook her head with a pucker of her pickled lips and wouldn't tell us any more.

The biggest stroke of luck was that the supply ship was due the very next morning. We didn't know *how* big a stroke of luck—we missed Mummy and the others by just a couple of hours.

The saddest thing was saying goodbye to the dogs. I'd miss Mayhem and Monster, Fluffy and Buster—all of them.

Goody-Two-Shoes cried. *Again.*

Captain Smudge wound up being a crusty old sailor who was not thrilled to take eight kids aboard his steamer. Still, he agreed to do it as a favor to Mrs. Keeper.

Even once we were on his ship, though, he kept trying to talk us out of going to Isle X.

"You'll be disappointed," he said. But he wouldn't ever explain why.

◆ ◆ ◆

Now is the time to tell you about all the great and amazing adventures we had aboard the *Sinbad*. How pirates attacked the ship and we only escaped by racing through a pod of whales, and about the iceberg that almost smashed into us. In the years since these events happened, I have told these tales to many such as yourself. But I was always lying.

To be honest—which I do hate being—the whole trip was pretty boring. Again! A surprising amount of adventuring is boring. That's why you have to make so much stuff up.

The secret to making up stuff is to give your stories a hint of truth. Capt. Smudge—salty dog that he was—told us all kinds of tales of his life on the high seas, including that one about the pirates and the pod of whales. And we did *see* a whale.

(Well, I *think* we saw a whale. It was dark. And it was far away.)

And not only had his ship almost been sunk by icebergs, but the *Sinbad* had been the first boat on the scene when the *Titanic* went down, and Capt. Smudge had personally rescued hundreds of passengers!

It was only when he told us about the time a giant squid swiped him off the deck of the *Sinbad* and he only escaped its clutches because a German U-boat torpedoed the monster that it occurred to me that maybe—*just* maybe—the captain wasn't being entirely truthful himself.

Which made me like him even more.

Because I did like him, and he liked us. *Until.*

Until he saw the graffiti on the deck of the *Sinbad*.

IF YOU READ THIS NOTE, DON'T FRET OR FEAR. IT ONLY MEANS THE NO-GOOD 9 WUZ HERE!

His face went all twitchy, and I thought his pipe was going to blow out of his mouth.

"I think it looks kinda nice," I said.

Wrong thing to say.

Capt. Smudge was so furious, he threatened to leave all of us on an ice floe. "And I *will* if you don't make that disappear!"

As we scrubbed off the paint, we tried to figure out who kept doing the graffiti.

"O.K., I admit it," I said. "It was *me.*"

But no one believed me. In fact, my copping to it just made them all sure I *hadn't* done it.

The Rude seemed like the obvious culprit, but he swore it wasn't him, and he was probably the most honest of us all.

The other natural suspect was the Hooligan, because of the way WUZ was spelled.

"But you think he knows how to spell *means*?" the Cruel said.

"Oh, *that's* what that word is!" the Hooligan said.

So if not them, who *was* doing it?

We didn't have time to figure it out, however, because from the fore of the ship we heard

"Island ho!"

So yes, I lied in the title. This chapter was *not* a great and amazing adventure. The great and amazing adventure was about to begin.

31. ARRIVAL ON ISLE X

"*Island ho!*" the first mate yelled again. But where the *ho* was the island?

All I could see was a black cloud on the horizon.

"That's it," Capt. Smudge said. "*Inside* the black cloud."

Which wasn't a cloud. It was smog, coming out of the giant smokestacks that rose up all across the island. Isle X looked just like

"Home," the Hooligan said. "It looks like Pittsburgh."

"We came all this way just to go to another *Pittsburgh*?" the Rude said.

"Except they don't make steel here," the Brat said. "They make toys. Now let's get to hiding."

This was our plan: to hide inside the boxes and sacks of supplies bound for Isle X. After getting off-loaded and stored in the warehouse where Capt. Smudge told us the cargo went, we would sneak out and find Santa's workshop. Then we would play with the toys, tell off Santa, and get *back* on board the *Sinbad* the next time it came. In a month.

Reading it now, it sounds like *another* horrible plan. But when we were talking about it on the ship, it sounded swell.

A deafening steam whistle sounded, and we hurried to get into our hiding places. I wanted to get inside the crate marked *pillows*, but the Rude beat me to it, so I wound up hiding in a sack of coffee instead.

The biggest problem—other than the smell of the beans—was that the moment after I got picked up, I got dropped.

"OOF, this one is heavy!" I heard someone—some *elf*?—say.

Inside the sack, I had to bite my lip not to yell

OUCH!

Then, two people—*more* elves?—picked up the burlap sack, and it was all I could do not to bust out laughing because I was getting grabbed by the ribs and knees and armpits and all those little elf hands tickled like heck.

Then I got pitched through the air, which—for a second—felt great, like I was flying!

And then

SLAM!

I landed in a mountain of other coffee sacks.

Now it was all I could do not to moan, but the sound of other voices and stuff getting moved around kept me scared enough that I was able to stay quiet, and then there *was* quiet, until I head a voice say

"One for nine?"

And we all said

"Nine for one!"

and got out of our hiding places.

The Hooligan was white as a ghost.

The barrel of flour was probably *not* the best place to hide.

We found ourselves standing in the middle of a giant, dark warehouse. It was set up like a kind of store, with each product laid out on shelves or the floor and marked with a number. Or was it a price?

As we tried to figure out exactly what kind of place

this was, a sudden BOOMING voice exploded into the room! I would've jumped out of my skin if it wasn't so well connected to my body.

—BZZT!—*Fellow elves! The supply ship has arrived! Please come to the market at eighteen hundred hours. Santa tokens and only Santa tokens are redeemable. Elves more than twenty tokens in debt will be allowed no credit!—*
BZZT!—

It was coming from a loudspeaker attached to the ceiling, and we realized that we were *in* the market—and it was about to get invaded by all of Santa's elves. We had to make like a tree and leave!

Opening the back door carefully, we snuck out of the gloomy warehouse. The world outside, however, was even more gloomy than the one inside.

A thick fog of coal smoke swallowed us up, and I had to hold back a cough. Streetlamps were blurry through the haze, and it was tough to see anything but shapes. It was spooky! Afraid of getting cut off from the group, I grabbed onto the shirt of the Ninester in front of me.

"If you want to keep your hands, I suggest you get them *off* of me!"

Oops—the shirt I grabbed should *not* have been the Cruel's.

Even if you *could* see where you were going, it would've been easy to get lost. The place was a maze of tall brick walls, all of the buildings identical.

Eventually, we came out into an open square.

"This looks nothin' like you told us it would," the Rude said to the Know-It-All. "Where are the gingerbread houses? Where's the winter wonderland?"

"Forget the stupid gingerbread houses," the Brat said. "Where are the *toys*?"

"Uh, I think maybe they're in there," the Hooligan said. He was pointing to a red neon sign across the smoggy plaza that read

TOY FACTORY

with a large blinking arrow pointing down.

32. THE TOY FACTORY

It all sounds too easy, but there was one problem. The Toy Factory was *teeming* with worker elves, which we could see through the windows.

But then it *wasn't* a problem, because a steam whistle

BLEW

our eardrums apart and out of the factory poured a flood of elves!

They weren't dressed like you'd expect an elf to dress, with pointy shoes and bright red-and-green hats and stuff. Instead, they had on plain blue overalls, like a factory worker anywhere would wear.

If we could see *them*, they could see *us*. But not a one of them turned in our direction. They all just wanted to get to that market.

"I can't wait to get some oranges!" one said.

"And the newest issue of *Black Mask*!" another said.

Once the last elf left, we just had to figure out how to break in.

The Hooligan wanted to smash a window, but the sound might blow our cover. The Thief spotted an open window, but it was high off the ground. While the Brat and the Cruel argued over the best way to climb up to it, Goody-Two-Shoes tried the front door.

It was unlocked.

"I guess there ain't much crime in Santaland," the Rude said.

"Well, there's about to be!" the Thief said.

Inside, the factory was *huge*.

At the entrance was a wall of punch cards beside a time clock and a changing area with work smocks and gloves. Stretching out beyond was a factory floor like you see in the newsreels, with assembly lines and massive steam-powered machines.

But where were the toys?

The only ones we could find were lying on the workbenches half-made.

"This can't be *it*," the Rude said. "Can it?"

As we tried to figure out what to do next, we heard "Humans!"

We weren't alone!

"Human children!"

Where was the voice coming from?

"What are you *doing* here?"

However scared we might've been, this quivering mystery person sounded downright terrified.

"It's comin' from under there," the Rude said, pointing below a worktable.

A pair of very frightened elf eyes peered out from the shadows below.

"You can't be here!" the half-hidden elf said. "Oh no, oh *dear*!"

"Who are *you*?" Goody asked, bending down to talk to him.

"Who am I? Who am I?" the elf said. "Who are *you*, is the question!"

Goody went to answer, but he cut her off.

"I'm an elf, is who I am. *I* belong here! I make toys!"

"But why are you *still* h-h-here?" the Know-It-All said. "All the other elves left for the m-m-market."

"And why are you under that workbench?" the Thief said.

Embarrassed, the elf came out.

"Even if I went to the market, I couldn't buy anything," he said. "I haven't been paid in weeks because I'm always behind on my work. That's why I'm here—to finish these toy airplanes. But look at them all!" He held out his hands to his workbench, full of little airplane parts. "It drives me crazy, trying to put these things together. There are always parts left over and parts I can't find. That's why they call me Lefty—because I'm so terrible at assembling this stuff, it's like I have two left hands."

"I'm left-handed, too," I said.

"But *I'm* not!" he said.

And neither was I.

"I didn't know an elf could be terrible at toy making," the Rude said.

"Who said *that*?" Lefty said, offended. "I was excellent at toy making back when we made them by hand. Why, I could carve a wooden toy in no time at all. It's this *factory* toy making that I'm no good at!"

He shook himself.

"But why am I explaining *myself*?" he said. "*You're* the ones who don't belong here!"

So we explained why we were there. (More or less, anyway.)

Lefty said he was sorry that we were all on the Naughty List. "But you still have to leave! You're not allowed on Isle X—no humans are. There are international laws and treaties against it! And besides, Santa will be furious if he finds out there are human children here!" Lefty shuddered at the thought of it. "Santa *hates* children!"

"How can Santa hate children?" Goody said.

"Never mind that!" Lefty said. "However you came, you have to leave the same way!"

When the Brat explained that we had come on the monthly supply ship, Lefty held his head in his hands.

"That is *not* good. No, that is not good at all."

"Look, we came all this way," the Rude said. "Can't we just play with some toys a *little*, and then we'll get out of your hair? We promise!"

"Yeah, we promise!" we all said.

Lefty wavered. He didn't *want* to let us, but he finally said O.K.

His agreeing *might* have had something to do with a tiny little fib I told about a rare blood disease and Goody-Two-Shoes only having two weeks left to live. When a tear came to the elf's eye, I felt bad. But I had to do it, right?

"You can play with the toys, but only for five minutes," Lefty said. "And then do you **promise** to leave?"

"We promise!" we said.

Making us *all* a bunch of liars.

33. PLAYTIME!

Lefty quickly solved the mystery of where all the toys were.

"As soon as they're finished, they get brought in here," he said, walking to a gigantic sliding door at the back of the factory. With an effort, he pulled it open to reveal a whole other building—a massive warehouse filled to the rafters.

With toys.

TOYS!

"Now, let me show you kids around a little," Lefty said.

We listened to the elf for about three seconds.

Then we all went **C-R-A-Z-Y**.

There were cap guns and pogo sticks and bicycles and toy soldiers and model trains! And Erector sets! And—*wow!*—a whole wall of play swords! And then I saw the sporting supplies.

Bats and balls and mitts and catcher's masks and boxing gloves and punching bags!

My family never could afford *any* of this stuff! We played stickball in the streets with broom handles because no one had bats. But here was the mother lode!

I tried one after the other. First the Babe Ruth model,

then the Ty Cobb, then Jimmie Foxx, and Lou Gehrig! I tossed the balls up and banged them off the walls, the ceiling, and—*whoops!*—through a window.

CRASH!

"I didn't do that!" I said.

But no one was listening.

Well, no one except Lefty. He was hollering for us all to stop, but I pretended not to hear him.

What I needed was someone to play ball with. But where had all the others gone?

I went searching through the aisles and found the Rude unbundling bales of play money. "I'm rich, I'm rich!" he said, throwing bills in the air. "Look at me, I'm Sparky Von Brat III! Now you have to do everything I say!"

The Brat might have been angry, but he was too busy putting together a massive train set.

Neither of them wanted to play baseball.

The Thief zipped by on a bright red bike.

"*Heydoyouwanna* . . ." I called to her, but she was gone.

I next asked the Know-It-All, but he had found the books. There were stacks of books, great towering *cliffs* of books.

"LOOK!" he said, pointing at one twenty-foot-high wall of them. "Nothing but Tarzans!"

The book aisle was the *last* place I wanted to be, so I left as soon as possible. The Thief zipped right by me going the other way on a bright *blue* bike.

"*Heydoyouwanna* . . ." I called, but she was gone again.

Goody-Two-Shoes was into the arts and crafts supplies. She had glue, paper, paints, brushes—you name it. "There are so many different colors of paint, I can't believe it!"

I didn't even bother asking her. The Hooligan maybe?

"Forget baseball!" he said. "Let's play soldier—or *gangster*! Look at this!" He went to a huge pile of cap boxes, ripped one open, and put a roll in a cap gun.

POP!

the gun went as it struck the cap.

"Take *that*, nice kids of the world!" he said, smoke rising from the cap gun.

POP!

"And *that*!"

POP POP POP!

The Thief zipped right by me on a bright *orange* bike. And . . .

I didn't bother.

The only one left was the Cruel. She was sitting in the middle of about five hundred dolls with glass eyes and blinking eyelashes that fluttered open and closed.

"Aren't you too . . ." I was about to say *old to play with that stuff*, but she shot me a look that made me think the better of it. ". . . lucky to have found those dolls!"

"You lied to me!" Lefty the elf said. "All of you! I never should have let you come in here! How will we ever clean all this up? And the noise you're making! Someone will come! And then you'll be in trouble! *Big* trouble!"

"What trouble?" I said. "We haven't done anything wrong."

"Haven't done anything wrong? Haven't done any-thing *wrong*?" Lefty said, sputtering. "Do you have any idea how many laws you've broken? Trespassing, break-ing and entering. And stealing!"

"We haven't stolen anything!"

"What about her?" he said, pointing to the Thief.

Finally off the bikes, the Thief had started stuffing toys under her shirt. It looked like she was pregnant. With triplets.

"And is that . . . *graffiti*?"

On one wall, it read

THANK YOU, NICE KIDZ,
YOU'RE MY-T FINE,
TO SHARE YER TOYZ
WITH THE NO-GOOD 9!

Who kept doing that?

At the moment, I didn't care. I started hitting base-balls off the walls again, which *really* drove Lefty crazy.

"I bet that girl isn't even dying! You lied about every-thing, didn't you? Ohhh, you really *are* nothing but a bunch of no-good Naughty Listers! I should never have *trusted* you! Oh no, oh dear . . ."

I was *just* about to start feeling guilty again and stop when

"Candy canes!"

Candy canes?

I followed the sound of the Hooligan's voice and found him standing in a crate full of nothing but CANDY CANES!

We all descended upon them, and began tearing open more and more boxes.

There were CARAMELS.

And LICORICE whips.

And CHOCOLATE.

And BUBBLE GUM.

And CARAMELS—did I mention them? (I *love* caramels.)

And ROCK CANDY.

And TAFFY.

We grabbed fistfuls, which became mouthfuls. There was *so* much of it, we just started throwing it at each other.

Candy fight!

Then we *really* went crazy. In fact, we got downright delirious.

On roller skates.

And pogo sticks.

And then I found the fireworks.

Oh, but I just *loved* fireworks!

I took out a pair of Roman candles and lit them, holding one in each hand as they spit out fountains of sparks.

"No!" Lefty hollered. "Not the fireworks! Do NOT play with the fireworks!"

"What fireworks?" I said. "I'm not playing with any fireworks."

"Yes, you *are*!" the elf shouted at me. "They're in your hands!"

"No, they're not!" I said. And then I did something pretty dumb.

I threw them away.

And I didn't even look where I was throwing them. Which wound up being—unfortunately—right into that big pile of cap gun cap boxes.

"**NO!**" Lefty yelled. "Not *that* way!!"

But it was too late.

34. AN ACCIDENT THAT WAS KIND OF MY FAULT

POP!

POP POP!

POP POP **POP POP POP POP!**

It sounded like a war in here!

I rushed to stamp out the fire, but it was too much. Red-orange cap gun rolls were flying around my head like confetti in a parade.

The other No-Good Ninesters realized what was happening and rushed to help.

But then something *really* bad happened.

A flaming roll of caps landed in the pile of dolls the Cruel had been playing with, and

FWOOM!

the hair ignited, and the toy warehouse seemed to catch fire everywhere at once.

Lefty pulled the fire alarm. A siren began to wail, drowning out the sound of explosions.

We ran. All of us made it out O.K., except for some coughing.

"Fireworks!" the Cruel said to me once we were safely outside. "You had to play with the *fireworks*?"

She then called me a bunch of not-very-nice names.

And the Hooligan slugged me on the shoulder.

What really hurt, though, was the way Goody-Two-Shoes was looking at me in disappointment.

"I'm sorry," I said, but then caught myself. "I mean, I am *not* sorry. Meaning I really am sorry."

The Hooligan slugged me again.

Elves began to arrive. They looked at the flaming building, horrified and confused, and then at us, and got even *more* confused.

Together with the elves, we watched the fire grow bigger

and the roof cave in

and one of the sides of the building fall down.

The Elf Fire Brigade finally arrived, its ancient fire wagon pulled by a couple of reindeer. They didn't even bother hosing down the toy warehouse because it was too far gone, so they turned their hoses on the Toy Factory, which was now on fire, too. But it didn't help.

Yes. You read that right. We—*I*—burned down Santa's toy factory.

I know it says that on the book jacket, but still, it's pretty shocking when you actually *read* it, isn't it?

35. ONE LAST CHAPTER IN THIS SORRY EPISODE

Standing there, looking at their factory ablaze, most of the worker elves were frozen in stunned silence. A couple of them cried.

Then came the sound of a loud, booming voice from the back of the crowd.

"What—what is going on here? What HAPPENED?" the voice thundered. "Let me through! Let me THROUGH!"

Then we saw him. And it was really *him*. The red suit,

the hat, the long white beard—everything but the *ho-ho-hos*.

Santa!

I have to admit, I was starstruck.

As for Santa, *well* . . . he seemed pretty darn upset.

"WHAT!" he screamed, seeing the fire. "WHAT IS GOING ON HERE! WHAT HAPPENED TO MY FACTORY!?!"

Another wall collapsed, and everyone jumped back amidst the sparks and smoke and flames.

"It's gone! My factory is GONE!" Santa said. He was apoplectic. "WHO is responsible for this? **WHO**?!"

The crowd of elves parted, and pointed back at *us*.

Santa stared in our direction for a moment. He shook his head and blinked his eyes like he was trying to break out of a hallucination.

"Are you . . . *children*?" Santa said, walking closer to us and squinting. "HUMAN children?"

"Geez, we sure are sorry about the fire, Mistuh Santa, sir," the Hooligan said, shaking his head at the shame of it all. "It sure is a tough break."

"Yes, we're *very* sorry," Goody said. "We didn't mean for anything bad to happen. We just came to play with the toys."

"The toys . . ." the Rude said, nodding.

"You . . . *children* . . . burned my factory down? Because you came to play with . . . the *toys*?" Santa said. "Don't you know that NO ONE gets to play with the toys before CHRISTMAS! Why couldn't you all just *WAIT?!*"

"Because we wouldn't have gotten any!" the Brat said, going into tantrum mode. "We're on the Naughty List!"

"**NAUGHTY LISTERS!**" A look of realization swept over Santa's face. "That explains EVERYTHING! You did this on PURPOSE!"

"No! It wasn't like that at all," the Rude said, but Santa didn't want to hear it.

"My beautiful factory—my life's work!—it's ruined! **RUINED!** And all by a bunch of rotten NAUGHTY LIST miscreants who ought to—

"who ought to—

"*who ought to—*"

Santa clutched his chest. His eyes rolled back in his head. And he dropped to the ground

THUD!

Lefty ran to try and revive him. But he couldn't.

"Uh, f-f-fellers," the Know-It-All said. "I think we just k-k-k-killed Santa Claus."

◆ ◆ ◆

Meanwhile . . .

Maybe now would be a good time to check in with Mummy and the Truant Officer, don't you think?

The only thing is that they weren't doing anything even remotely interesting.

They still had a whole week to wait for the *Sinbad* to return to Black Tickle, at which point they would try convincing Capt. Smudge to take them to Isle X like he took us.

About the only way for them to pass the time was to play cards. Unfortunately for the Truant Officer, the Vainglorious couldn't follow any card game other than war, and even then he forgot the rules.

"The higher card wins. That is the *only* rule!"

What I don't get is how Mummy kept Mr. and Mrs. Keeper from clueing in my archenemy to the fact that they were prisoners in their own lighthouse. Part of it, maybe, was that the Brothers Jack never let the Keepers out of their sight. A bigger part, more likely, is that the Truant Officer wasn't any brighter than the Vainglorious when it came to following what the heck was going on.

EPISODE SIX:
PRISONERS OF ISLE X

36. UNWELCOME GUESTS

Let me begin this episode by making one thing very clear: We did **not** kill Santa Claus.

It wasn't *our* fault the man didn't take better care of himself. He never exercised or went to the doctor for an annual checkup, and do you know that he *smoked*? He had a pipe in his mouth all day long.

Frankly, it was a miracle Santa hadn't dropped dead sooner.

And—as it wound up—he wasn't even dead.

We *thought* he was dead, but he had only fainted.

(Or suffered a very minor heart attack.)

As you can imagine, there was a major hubbub among the elves after Santa collapsed. Unfortunately for him, the Toyland ambulance wasn't much better than its fire truck, but it did eventually manage to get Santa to Dr. Elf.

It was a pretty tense few hours there while we waited to hear whether or not the big guy pulled through.

And to see whether or not the Toy Factory would ever stop burning.

Have you ever had someone hate you? Look at you with eyes like they wanted to burn a hole right through you?

Well, that's pretty much the way every elf was looking at us.

We breathed a huge sigh of relief when we heard the crackle of the loudspeaker and it said

—**BZZT!**—*Excellent news, fellow elves! Santa has survived! Rejoice! Rejoice!*—**BZZT!**—

Rejoicing, however, seemed like the last thing the elves wanted to do. In fact, they didn't seem to care one way or the other *what* happened to Santa.

Of course, none of them would talk to us, so what did *we* know?

Actually, that's not true—Lefty would talk to us. And thank goodness he did, because otherwise we would have had no place to sleep. Not that the old abandoned elf barracks where he stowed us away were so great. For one thing, they were falling apart. For another, they were built elf height.

"*OWTCH!*"

The Hooligan kept banging his head on the tops of the doorways.

"*OWTCH!*"

"How about you try ducking, genius?" the Cruel said.

The beds were pretty crappy, too. They were old and brittle and too short for our legs. Well, except for the legs of one of us.

"I don't know *what* you all are complaining about," the Rude said. "This is comfy!"

"That's because you're short," the Hooligan said. "Now geddup on the top bunk, twerp."

The Rude refused to go, so the Hooligan grabbed him. As soon as he did, the Rude let out a very loud—and smelly—fart.

"You want the bed now?"

The Hooligan muttered something and climbed to the upper bunk. He swung himself onto the bed and

THWOOP!

crashed right through the mattress, landing on top of the Rude. Then the two of them went crashing

THWOOP!

right through the bottom bunk.

"It's like rooming with Laurel and Hardy," the Brat grumbled, turning over in his bunk.

I'd explain who Laurel and Hardy were, but right now I'm too tired just *remembering* how tired I was. I'm going to sleep!

37. WHAT I WROTE AFTER I WOKE UP

"So w-w-w-what's going to happen to us?" the Know-It-All asked Lefty.

Lefty shrugged.

"It's up to the boss," he said.

The thing was, Santa still hadn't come out of his house, which stood out on a cliff at the far edge of the island.

On the plus side, at least the fire was finally out.

—BZZT!—All elves report for clean-up duty on the factory at oh eight hundred hours!—BZZT!—

"O.K., Ninesters," Goody-Two-Shoes said, clapping her hands, "let's go pitch in!"

"Aw, do we *hafta*?" the Hooligan said.

"Yeah, why should we?" the Rude said. "What else have the elves got to do anyway? They can't make toys anymore."

"It's our fault," Goody said, "so we have to help."

"It's not *our* fault. It's *his* fault!" the Hooligan said, pointing at me.

I shrank.

It *was* my fault, and I felt really bad about it. There

might be no Christmas this year—because of *me*. Maybe the Truant Officer was right about me being a *negodnik* menace to society.

"Don't say that about yourself!" Goody said.

"Yeah, you shouldn't feel bad," the Rude said. "At least we got some time in the Toy Factory before your screw-up. I'll never forget it!"

"Me, I'm glad you burned it down," the Brat said. "Just think—*we* got to play with the toys of the nice kids of the world and *they* never will!"

We all went to the ruins of the factory, which were still smoking. Only one wall was left standing, the one with the graffiti on it.

"Who keeps d-d-doing that?" the Know-It-All said.

We looked at the Rude.

"It *still* ain't me!" he said.

Although the elves continued not to talk to us—they could really hold a grudge—we did our best to help haul off the rubble and debris. As we worked, we uncovered lots and lots of toys. Or what was left of them.

"Hey, lookit! Pop guns!" the Hooligan said. But they were all melted together.

We found the glass eyes of teddy bears scattered everywhere and some sad-looking dolls, with porcelain heads cracked like eggs and bald from their hair being singed off.

We shoveled the debris into sacks, which got put

onto reindeer sleighs and dumped into the sea.

Did I mention the flying reindeer?

It was pretty amazing how they could fly and all, but once you got used to them, it wasn't such a big deal. And they were otherwise pretty disappointing.

For one thing, they didn't have names. There was no Dasher or Dancer, no Prancer or Vixen—just a herd of indistinguishable, unnamed, and kind of mangy reindeer. With fleas.

"How can fleas even survive in this cold?" the Brat said, plucking one off his neck.

"They're magic fleas, ya stupid!" the Rude said as a reindeer rubbed its head on his shirt.

It went on like this for days. At the end of each day, we were covered in black soot and exhausted and hungry.

Back at the barracks, Lefty made us dinner, which was the same thing as lunch, which was the same thing as breakfast.

Gruel.

Despite its awful-sounding name, gruel is just a kind of oatmeal. It doesn't *have* to taste terrible.

Unfortunately for us, in addition to being a terrible toy maker, Lefty was a terrible cook. So it *did* taste terrible.

Still, we gobbled it up, because anything tastes better than starving.

"So what would happen if Santa *did* die?" the Rude

said, his mouth chock-full of gruel. "Would Christmas be kaput? Over forever?"

"Oh, no!" Lefty said. "Christmas will *never* be over. Lots of Santas have died."

Lefty explained that "Santa" was just their term for the chief elf. When a Santa died, a conclave of elves elected a new one. The present Santa, Lefty said, was the one who had changed everything.

"Before him, we made the toys by hand in small workshops. It was so much fun! But he bulldozed the old cottages down and built that steam-powered factory and all the other industrial buildings. The only thing he cares about is making more and more toys," Lefty said, shaking his head and scraping the bottom of his bowl with a spoon. "It used to be that kids only got *one* thing for Christmas, but this Santa wants to give them everything they ask for."

"Except the naughty ones," the Cruel said.

"Oh yeah," Lefty said. "He sure doesn't like the naughty ones."

In addition to setting up the factory, Santa had put his right-hand elf, Amanuensis, in charge of a team of elves who kept tabs on kids. Amanuensis was the keeper of the Naughty and Nice Lists, and went with Santa on Christmas night to tell him which kids got which toys, and which kids got coal. "When a page is done, he sets it on fire and leaves it to burn in the fireplace while he and Santa go up the chimney."

"So *that*'s how the Naughty List got left at my h-h-h-h—"

The Know-It-All couldn't get the word out before

—BZZT!—Attention, HUMAN children! Please report to the TOWER at oh nine hundred hours tomorrow morning. Repeat: ALL HUMAN children must report to the Tower at oh nine hundred hours!—BZZT!—

We looked at each other.

"Guess we'll find out what's gonna happen to us *now*," the Rude said. And let out a stinky gruel-fueled belch.

38. THE EYE IS WATCHING YOU

The Square, which stood at the center of Isle X, was lined with brick buildings. At one end lay the ruins of the Toy Factory; at the opposite end rose the Tower, which dominated the Square like some kind of cathedral. At the peak of the Tower, a glass clock showed its face to all of Isle X. The elves called it the Eye, and it served as the central office of Santa's entire industrial operation. At night, the Eye glowed whenever Amanuensis was working inside. And he was *always* working inside.

"Amanuensis is the one who makes the announcements," Lefty told us as we walked. "He runs pretty much everything for Santa."

Mounted right below the 6 of the clock was a fat loud-speaker, a big mouth to go with the Tower's all-seeing Eye. From behind it, a thick web of wires spread out to connect it to all the other loudspeakers across Isle X.

I felt a shiver, and it wasn't because of the wind.

"So you go in through *there*," Lefty said, pointing to a heavy iron-and-wood door at the base of the Tower.

"You're not c-c-coming with us?" the Know-It-All said.

Lefty shook his head furiously and said there was NO WAY he was going in there.

"I'm afraid of Amanuensis," he said. "He keeps a list for elves, too!"

Lefty hurried back across the Square.

I was ready to follow him when the Cruel pressed the button beside the door. A moment later there was a

ZZZ-ZZZ

and the door opened.

"Wow, that's jake!" the Rude said. "A magic door!"

"It's not magic, it's automated," the Know-It-All said, and pointed to the mechanism that controlled its swing.

"Killjoy," the Rude grumbled.

There was only one way to go—up—so we climbed the stairs, which went even higher than the stairs of the lighthouse.

At the top, we found a room that looked more like it was for managing war than managing Christmas. A giant globe of the world sat in front of the one window in the room—the clock face of the Eye—and there were maps with thousands of pins stuck in them hanging on all four walls. Below the maps were filing cabinets. So *many* filing cabinets!

In the middle of it all sat two heavy oak desks, one enormous, the other just a little bit less enormous. On them were brass nameplates that read SANTA CLAUS and AMANUENSIS.

Santa was seated at his desk looking over blueprints, dressed in his red suit. Behind him stood another elf, this one dressed like a factory boss in a dark suit and waistcoat. This was Amanuensis.

Neither of them acknowledged us, until:

"So what's in all the filing cabinets, fellers?"

Both Santa and Amanuensis looked up through their reading glasses at the Rude like he was something they needed to spit out.

"The List," Amanuensis said coldly.

"Mr. Santa, sir," Goody-Two-Shoes said. "We want to apologize again for everything that happened. We never meant—"

Santa held up a hand to stop her. "The *List,*" he said to Amanuensis. "Read them the *List.*"

Amanuensis smiled.

The elf walked over to one of the filing cabinets. He stood at one for a minute, pulling out folder after folder until he had a great big stack that he dropped on his desk with a

THUD!

Amanuensis cleared his throat and opened the first folder.

"Henry Alistair 'Sparky' Chaudfront III," he began.

We all turned to look at the

"BRAT. Age twelve. On list: seven years. Naughty activities include talking back to parents, yelling at servants, insulting teachers, and once telling a storekeeper *My father can buy and sell you.*"

Santa shook his head disapprovingly from side to side while the Brat's face went the color of raw steak.

"Naughty List status," Amanuensis declared. "**Permanent!**"

The elf picked up an even thicker folder.

"John 'Johnny' Colson. RUDE."

"Right here!" The Rude raised his hand and grinned.

Amanuensis grunted.

"Age eleven. On list: four years. Naughty activities include swearing, obscene gestures, talking back to adults, chewing with mouth open, urinating in public, and farting in public."

"I did do all that," the Rude said proudly. "Plus a lot more you missed!"

"*Status*," Amanuensis said, "was annual review. Now, *permanent*!"

He marked a big *X* on the page and shut the folder. The next one was

"Luigi 'Looie' Curidi. LIAR. Age twelve."

Gulp.

Amanuensis went through a lengthy list of my Naughty crimes, to the end of which he said could now be added burning down the Toy Factory.

"Which I still feel really, really bad about!"

Santa harrumphed.

The only one who did not seem to be feeling the slightest bit bad about any of her Naughty crimes was the Cruel. The list of things she had done was so long that Amanuensis just stopped and said, "You all get the idea."

The Cruel glowered at him in such a way that even Amanuensis looked cowed.

"Moving on, there's *this* one . . ." he said. He shook his head as he flipped through the pages in the folder. "This one was a *mistake*. You're not even supposed to *be* on the Naughty List."

"I knew it!" the Rude said. "I *knew* Miss Goody-Two-Shoes never did a naughty thing in her life!"

"You mean *her*?" Amanuensis said, crooking a finger at Goody. He let out a belly laugh. "Oh no, not her! She's been on the list for *years*."

The elf reached across his desk to a different file.

"Mimi Choice. VANDAL! Age twelve. On list: four years. Naughty activity includes vandalism by *graffiti*."

We all turned to Goody-Two-Shoes.

She shrank.

"It was *you*!" the Thief said.

"That's what the *V* stands for!" the Brat said. *"Vandal!"*

The Rude gave her a thumbs-up.

I was pretty impressed, too. I knew she fit in with the team.

For once, the only one not paying attention to Goody was the Know-It-All.

"But who then?" he asked the elf. *"Who* is on the Naughty List by m-m-m-mistake?"

Amanuensis looked at him like he was a moron.

"You!" he said. "One of the secretary elves got you mixed up with *another* twelve-year-old Peter Czaplynsky who lives in Sewickley, *Wisconsin*. Who would ever think there could be *two* humans with such a ridiculous name!"

"B-b-but," he stammered, "the list *says* I'm a know-it-all."

"Being a know-it-all doesn't get you on the Naughty List!" Santa interjected. He took his glasses off. "If only you had sent me a letter—a *petition*—we would've made a correction. In fact, I would have made a special delivery of all the toys you were missing!"

"But you're sure on the Naughty List *now*," Amanuensis said, and made a big mark in his folder. "***Forever!***"

The Know-It-All got his most pukeful look yet. I felt like I had to stand up and defend him. But I was beaten to the punch by—of all people—the Brat.

"But he *did* write a petition!" the Brat said. "And that's why he came up with this entire plan—to hand deliver it to you!"

"Show 'em!" the Hooligan said, slapping the Know-It-All on the back so hard that he almost fell over.

The Know-It-All fumbled through his pockets and started unfolding a piece of paper, stuttering and stammering. "I-i-it's about . . . well, the p-p-p-petition . . . it's not just for m-m-m-me, it's for all the children of the world, and how the N-N-N-Naughty List is not fair—"

"Not fair?" Santa thundered, cutting him off. "Not FAIR? Were you not LISTENING to what Amanuensis just read? To what you all have DONE? And then— instead of writing me a letter or attempting to better yourselves—you children ran away from home, snuck onto our island, and broke into our factory to play with what didn't belong to you. And then you BURNED it down!"

"Santa, calm down," Amanuensis said. "Before you have another heart attack."

"Let me FINISH!" Santa said, his face getting every bit as red as the Brat's ever got. (Well, *almost*.) "If what you children have done proves *anything*, it is how IMPORTANT the Naughty List is. Human children are horrible little monsters who must be given a reason to be good. The whole POINT of Christmas is to try and get you creatures to behave."

"*That's* the point of Christmas?" Goody-Two-Shoes said. "I thought it was peace on earth."

Santa scoffed at the thought.

The other kids kept trying to argue with Santa, but it was useless. He was just another adult who was never going to change his mind about anything, especially not because a bunch of kids told him to. Whether or not we were right made no difference.

What I wanted to know was what was going to happen to *us*. And if he was going to take us away in a flying sleigh.

Because that would be *aces*!

"No, you will NOT be leaving in one of my sleighs," Santa said. "You will go back the way you came. On the mail steamer. Once you are off this island, I suggest you go home to your parents and beg their forgiveness. But while you are HERE, you will keep working to try and clean up the mess you have created. You are dismissed!"

"But what about—" the Brat said.

"Dis"—Amanuensis cut him off—"**missed**."

39. THE BIG GOODBYE

I sure couldn't imagine begging my parents for forgiveness, but I did try hard to think about what it would be like to go home. To see my mom and dad, my brothers and sisters, my cousins, and—geez, it was exhausting just remembering them all!

It'd be nice to visit my family, but I couldn't picture *living* back there again. Sleeping on the floor of that tiny little apartment, ditching school, and waiting for the day when I had to go work in some crummy factory like my older brother Enzo—*if* I was lucky enough to get a job.

No, I did not want to go home. At least, not to *my* home.

Of course, none of the Ninesters wanted to go home, either. Mostly, it was understandable. The Rude lived in a lousy flophouse and worked two jobs, while the Hooligan was worried he'd wind up in prison like his older brother if he fell back in with his old gang. The Cruel's orphanage didn't sound like much fun, and it wasn't like *any* of us ever wanted to see Mummy Rummy again, least of all the Thief. The Brat would have to go back to boarding school, and who wants to *live* at *school*?

There were only a couple of kids I didn't really understand not wanting to go home. The Know-It-All said he
was scared of the whupping he'd get from his dad, but I
got beat up all the time and I still didn't get to live in a
nice house like his. Heck, he only had to share his room
with *one* sister!

And I still didn't get why Goody-Two-Shoes was
so afraid of her parents. Or why she had done all that
graffiti.

Of course, after the reading of the Naughty List, that
was all anyone wanted to ask her about. But she kept
mum.

The funny thing is, when she did talk about it, it was
me that she talked to. Maybe it was because I was a good
secret-keeper, or because if I did spill her secrets, no one
would believe me.

She did the graffiti, Goody said, because her parents
expected her to be perfect all the time.

I told her I didn't get it.

"My whole life has always been about making *them*
happy. So the only way to get back at them was to do
something they would hate."

She shrugged.

"That, plus I really like painting big signs on walls."

I nodded.

"Now I get it," I said, although I still didn't. I just
wanted to ask her the question that had been bothering

me since that first time we met her.

Why had she waited until her mom left the room to put her glasses on?

"Because my mother doesn't like me wearing glasses. She thinks they make me look ugly," Goody said. "She says that a girl's job is not to *see*, but to be *seen*."

And *now* I got it.

So we all had our reasons for not going home, but we had to go someplace. We just didn't know where.

Capt. Smudge and the *Sinbad* still weren't due back for another couple of weeks, but we were all antsy to go, what with how much the elves hated us and the way Santa worked us. He was always barking to do this better and clean up that faster.

It was while we were working that we heard a distant steam whistle blow.

One of the elves pointed out to sea. It was the mail steamer.

"The ship came early! The ship came early!" the elves chanted and cheered.

I got a tingle of excitement and then it hit me: We were about to leave.

I wasn't prepared for the moment to come so soon, and I felt a sudden stab of regret. It wasn't that I didn't want to get off this island—I did—it was more the feeling that we hadn't done what we had set out to do. I mean, nobody would say that the first mission of the No-Good

Nine was a rousing success, and I was worried that it would be our last and only one.

As it turned out, I shouldn't have been worrying about that.

What I *should* have been worrying about was why the heck the steamer was back two weeks early.

◆ ◆ ◆

Meanwhile . . .

From the Truant Officer's journal:

Mrs. Mummy's powers to persuade are remarkable. First with Bawdy Claude, then with the Keepers, and now with Smudge, the captain of the mail steamer.

She somehow managed to convince him to reverse his course and take us to Isle X, even though he wasn't supposed to go back for several weeks.

I suppose it is hard for anyone to say no to a mother in search of her daughter.

Even so, it is amazing that it has worked out. That we are here! As our ship pulls closer to the island and the horn blows, we see real live elves running to greet us on the dock.

And children.

40. A TRIO OF
UNPLEASANT SURPRISES

The first surprise came when I was standing on the dock watching the ship come in and I heard someone calling me.

"**Liar!**" came the voice from the boat. "There you are! My friend! And **Brat**! And **Cruel**! All of you!"

"Is that . . ." the Brat said.

"It *can't* be . . ." the Cruel said.

But it was.

The *Vainglorious*.

Have you ever had one of those moments when the world makes *no* sense?

It was impossible that he was on the mail steamer, and yet there he was, at the front of the deck, *waving* at us.

And then I heard another voice I knew.

"I told you before, Luigi Curidi," it said. "I *always* catch my man!"

It was my nemesis! The Truant Officer! But how could that *be*? The last time I saw him, he was with . . .

Oh, *right*. We had left the two of them together! But still, how could they have found us? It was impossible, it was—

"*No*," the Thief said.

She had just seen who else was on the ship.

"Oh no," the Thief said softly. "No, no, *no*."

I could see the gold tooth of that hideous smile glistening all the way from shore. I can *still* see it.

Can we *stop* this chapter and take a break? Please?

Because I still can't handle what happened.

41. WHAT HAPPENED

So, you can probably imagine what was going through my head—what was going through *all* of our heads. How, how, *how* did this happen?

Of course, you already know how these three jokers—plus the Brothers Jack—managed to get to Isle X. For us, however, there was a lot of explaining to do.

But before that came the big family reunion.

"My dear, dear daughter!" Mummy said, bursting into big sloppy fake tears and hugging the Thief. "I was so, so *worried*!"

In the grip of that headlock of a hug, the Thief looked like a rabbit caught in a dog's mouth—in shock. She wasn't moving and her eyes were wide and glassy.

I was in a little bit of shock myself.

"You came all this way *just* to take me back to school?" I said to my archenemy.

"This is not about skipping school," the Truant Officer said. He explained how busting up our "ring" was going to make him famous and that as a reward he would become a real policeman. "Maybe even an FBI agent!"

Then there was the Vainglorious.

"You must have all been so worried about me!" he said as he hugged each of us. "No need to worry anymore! I'm *fine*! It was just a terrible mistake at the train station!"

The rest of us looked at each other.

Could he really be this deluded?

"Yes, such a *terrible* mistake," I said. "We are *so* glad you found us."

Which was mostly a lie, but not totally. I myself was a little glad he was here. Because that meant there were finally *nine* of us.

We were the No-Good Nine for real!

"Can someone explain to *me* what's going on?" Santa said.

And here's where we got to the explaining part. Of course, a lot of it was a lie. At least, when it was Mummy Rummy doing the explaining it was a lie.

We *tried* to tell Santa that she was an evil bootlegger—that she had left us for *dead*!—but he wasn't having any of it.

You think **I'm** a good liar? Well, Mummy had Santa believing she was the most concerned mother who had ever walked the face of the earth. In fact, she blamed *us* for corrupting her daughter.

"These dirty-rotten Naughty Listers!" Santa said, shaking his head.

The Vainglorious wasn't helping our case, either.

"Oh, you guys! Always misunderstanding things," he said. "Maybe it's the language. Because Mummy is the *nicest* lady."

The Truant Officer vouched for her, too. He then told Santa that he'd take us back to the proper authorities in Pittsburgh and that we'd all likely wind up in reform school.

"That sounds like an excellent idea!" Santa said.

The idea of going to reform school sounded pretty bad—even worse than home—but not half as bad as where the Thief was headed.

"Don't you worry about this one, men," Mummy said, holding the Thief tight. "I'll set 'er back on the path of the straight and narrow. She won't be escaping from *me* again."

The Thief no longer had that glassy-eyed look. Her eyes were racing around like she was desperately searching for a way to escape.

In the meantime, there was one person on the ship that Santa was *not* happy with.

Capt. Smudge.

"How **dare** you bring these Naughty Listers to my island!" Santa yelled at him. "After all I've paid you over the years!"

"Oh, please don't be mad at 'im, Santa!" Mummy said. "'E is a sweet man 'oo thought 'e was *'elping* the children. And after all, 'e 'elped *me* come get my daughter. And 'e's going to take them away, too."

"The sooner the better," Santa grumbled.

"I 'ope not *too* soon," Mummy said. "I just don't think I can bear getting right back on that boat."

She held a hand to her forehead like she was a damsel in distress in some dopey movie.

"Well, I suppose you can stay for a day . . ." Santa said.

"And I would just *love* to see 'ow your operation works!" Mummy said, putting a hand on Santa's arm. "I 'ave a little manufacturing business myself. A . . . *baking* operation. Maybe you could give me some tips. I would love to see 'ow a *master* industrialist operates."

"Well, I certainly could," Santa said, puffing out his chest. "I suppose I *can* stand the sight of these Naughty Listers for one more day. In fact, I will treat you *all* to a dinner at my house! To show you how forgiving I can be."

"Does this mean you forgive me for burning down your factory?" I said.

Santa looked at me. His eyes narrowed. "It does not."

I didn't think so.

42. THE TOUR

Mummy, the two Jacks, and my archenemy were being given a tour of Isle X like they were some kind of visiting royalty.

"We actually *have* had the king of England here," Santa said. "Not to mention three presidents, Babe Ruth, Mark Twain, and the pope."

"And none of them have ever revealed the location of Isle X?" the Truant Officer asked. "Why not?"

"Because I'd put them on the Naughty List!" Santa said. "*HO HO HO!*"

Yeah, *ho ho ho*. It was all a big laugh for Santa now. Meanwhile, we were running out of time if we wanted to figure a way out of this mess.

Reform school?

That was *not* good.

"Well **I'm** not going," the Brat said. "Once we get on the ship, we'll overpower the Truant Officer and go our own way."

"But what about Mummy and the B-B-B-B-Brothers Jack?" the Know-It-All said. "They'll b-b-b-be on the ship, too!"

While we hung back and huddled over how to escape,

Santa was out front bragging about his factory.

"Now, don't get me wrong," he said to the Truant Officer and Mummy, "the factory burning down is a major setback. We may have to cancel Christmas this year all together."

Mummy gasped. "'Ow 'orrible!"

"Yes. But as you can see, we've already begun building a *new* factory, and by adding state-of-the-art machinery, our production will soar. By next Christmas, we should be able to make up for this year by giving children *double* what they ask for!"

"The *nice* ones," Amanuensis said, looking back at us with a sneer.

The Rude stuck out his tongue at him.

"All of this machinery—can it *only* be used to make toys?" Mummy said, all innocent voiced. "Or can any of it be changed over to make—oh, I don't know—a bottled grain-based beverage?"

The tour curved around to the top of the island, where the stables and reindeer pens were located. Coming back around, we arrived at the sleigh maker's workshop.

Walking in, Santa explained how they had phased out the old-fashioned wooden sleighs years ago. "Now all our models have modern steel suspensions and all-metal bodies. And instead of jingle bells, we use air horns."

BLANNNH!

he demonstrated.

The main sleigh—THE XMAS NITE SPECIAL—was enormous. The vehicle was as big as Mummy's trucks and then some, with different levels to store the toys and built-in ladders to get at them. How this massive hunk of metal ever got off the ground, I couldn't imagine.

"What an amazing delivery system you've put together, Mr. Claus," Mummy said.

"Oh please, call me Santa!"

While Mummy was *oohing* and *ahhing* over Santa's sleighs, I took my archenemy aside. He might have been my nemesis, but he wasn't a bad guy—not like Mummy. If only I could convince him what Mummy was *really* like, maybe I could convince him that he couldn't let her take the Thief.

But no matter what I told him about what Mummy had done to her—"She's not even really her daughter!"— he wouldn't believe he was being duped.

"Look," I said, "in all the time you've known me, have I *ever* lied to you?"

He looked at me like I was nuts.

"Yes," he said. "All the time!"

"That may be true," I said. "But I'm not lying *now*."

I couldn't get through to the Vainglorious either.

"Doesn't Mummy seem—oh, I don't know . . ." I said. *"Evil?"*

"You have her all wrong. She's a swell lady! The whole trip here she kept saying how much she wanted to get all of you back so she could teach you a lesson. See?" he said. "She's a *teacher*!"

They were *both* hopeless.

Walking back toward the Square, Mummy asked Santa how he got to be in charge and he explained the whole election process.

"Before that, I was just an elf like any other," Santa said. "But once I put on the suit, all the other elves had to do whatever I said."

"So you're saying *'ooever* wears that suit is absolutely, 100 percent in charge?" Mummy asked.

Santa nodded. "Elves like order. And we *never* break rules."

Mummy smiled her wicked gold-toothed smile.

The lady was just oozing evilness! How could these guys not *see* that?

43. WHAT'S FOR DINNER

After a demonstration of the public address system—in which Amanuensis sent a booming welcome out across Isle X to *our very special guests*—we exited the Eye by the back door and followed a path up a cliff that jutted out over the water. Here, the sea breeze blew away the coal smoke and you could finally *breathe*. At the very highest point of the cliff stood the final stop: Santa's house.

The house itself looked like it had been dropped there from somewhere else. Instead of red brick like everything else on the island, it was made of wood, and painted gray and black. It had slate roofs slanting from all different levels and angles, with round roof gables on the turrets and fancy ironwork. Cheerful it was not, but it *was* impressive, and the inside was a hundred times nicer than any of the elves' overcrowded workers' housing.

In the hall, Santa kicked off his boots and removed his coat, his hat, and—this was disturbing—his *beard*, which I hadn't realized was fake. He hung it on a hook in the hallway next to his outfit.

He then put on a smoking jacket, a fez, and a pair of slippers.

The house was full of incredible smells coming from the kitchen—*meat!*—and there was a phonograph playing opera records.

Santa re-stuffed his pipe, and Mummy joined him with a cigar in the wallpapered drawing room. While the two of them gabbed, the rest of us sat around in awkward silence until dinner got served.

And *what* a dinner!

One of the kitchen elves set a silver platter down in the middle of a long dining table dressed with fancy linens. There was a big juicy roast on it, and more kitchen elves brought more heaping trays full of mashed potatoes and creamed spinach and carrots and cabbage.

I had never seen a spread like this! I had to hold my mouth closed with my hand to keep the drool from spilling out.

"Who would like to say grace?" Santa said after he finished carving the roast.

Without skipping a beat, the Rude said

"Father, Son, and Holy Ghost,
Whoever eats fastest
Gets the most!"

And we all dug in.

It was not pretty, I can tell you that. But it wasn't *us* who were the most disgusting eaters—it was the elves.

Santa and Amanuensis dug in with their fingers and were licking the grease off of them and burping.

Santa saw how disgusted Goody-Two-Shoes was and said, "Slurping and burping is considered polite in elf society."

"I *like* this kind of polite!" the Rude said, and burped himself.

Goody was embarrassed that Santa had caught her being judgmental, so she tried to recover by saying, "This meat is delicious. Is it beef?"

"Oh, no," Santa said between loud chews. "It's reindeer."

The sound of everyone eating stopped with the clinking of forks hitting plates. We all looked at Santa.

"It's the only kind of meat we have up here," he said helplessly.

"I wonder if this one's Donner," Mummy said, taking another bite. "Donner for dinner! *AH-AH-AH!*"

The two Jacks laughed, too.

As well as the Rude.

"*What*? It's funny," he said as I elbowed him to quit it. "And reindeer *is* delicious." The Rude licked his fingers and reached for another piece.

I was still hungry, but I couldn't bring myself to eat any more Donner or Blitzen or whichever reindeer it was, so I just munched on mashed potatoes.

Meanwhile, Mummy kept peppering Santa with questions. Out of anyone else's mouth, I might not have thought they meant anything, but with Mummy, I was mighty suspicious. The one question she kept asking was:

"Are you sure the elves will follow *whoever* wears the big red suit?"

At the end of the meal, she and Santa went by the fire and started smoking again. (There was a *lot* of smoking in 1932, proving people were never very smart.) She then took out a bottle and poured something into Santa's glass.

"This is a little sample of what *I* make," Mummy said.

"I thought you were a baker," Santa said, sniffing at the glass. "This smells like liquor!"

"So it does," Mummy said, grinning. "And much like you with your toys, I am—'ow would you say it?—an exporter. *My* problem is getting my goods across the border. Your sleigh-and-chimney delivery system, 'owever, would be perfect for my rum-running. And I could make so *much* rum if I took over your factory."

Santa let out a jolly *HO-HO-HO!*

"Why do you laugh?" Mummy said.

"Because you're joking," Santa said. "You *are* joking, I hope."

Mummy assured him that she was not.

And that was when Santa got annoyed.

"Those sleighs are only for toys!" he thundered. "Not bootlegged liquor! And my factories! MY factories!" He got up, slammed down his glass, and pointed out the door. "It is time for you to LEAVE, madam!"

"I am not the one 'oo's leaving," Mummy said.

She snapped her fingers, and the Jacks got up from the table, each holding a gun.

Where had they been hiding those things?

"Mrs. Mummy!" the Truant Officer said, rising to his feet. "What is the meaning of this?"

"Sit down and shut up, you fool," she said, pushing him back into his seat. "These flying reindeer and magic sleighs will make me the most powerful bootlegger in the world! And with this factory and these worker elves, I'll make liquor faster than Coca-Cola makes sugar water!"

Confused—stunned—shattered, the Truant Officer looked from one gun to the other. "Are you taking us . . ." he said, *"prisoner?"*

Mummy laughed.

"That would be a *yes*," I said to my archenemy.

"You'll never get away with this!" Santa said, exploding. "Why—why—the elves will RISE up and free me!"

"Oh, really?" Mummy said. She walked into the hall and put on the Santa outfit.

"I always wanted a beard! *AH-AH-AH!*" she said as she put on the final item.

She looked ridiculous.

"But you can't be Santa," Santa said. "There's never been a WOMAN Santa before!"

At that, Mummy's good cheer vanished. "If there's *one* thing Mummy 'ates, it's being told I can't do something," she said, dark and menacing. "The only thing I 'ate *more* is when someone tells me I can't do something because I am a *woman!*"

"AMANUENSIS!" Santa said. "Tell her it won't work!"

Amanuensis looked to Santa, then looked to Mummy, dressed as Santa. He shrugged. "She wears the suit."

He turned to Mummy.

"So, what do you want me to do, Santa?"

44. MUMMY-DAUGHTER RELATIONSHIP

Before we end this episode, I have to tell you something—something *shocking*—that happened before we left Santa's house.

Which, to be accurate, had just become Mummy's house. But never mind that.

Mummy told Amanuensis to go lock us up. Us being not just the No-Good Nine, but Santa and the Truant Officer, too.

The Vainglorious didn't have to come, but he finally saw Mummy for who she really was.

"You can't do this to my friends, Mummy!" he said. "If you're putting *them* in jail, then you have to put *me* in jail, too!"

"Gladly!" Mummy said, and shoved him toward the rest of us.

The Vainglorious turned out to be a lot more loyal than any of us could've imagined. But still not so smart.

That wasn't the shocking part, though.

The shocking part was the Thief.

"What about me?" she said.

"What *about* you?" Mummy said. "You should be thankful I even let you live!"

"The No-Good Nine may be *his* friends, but they're not *mine*. And they never were," the Thief said. "I want to stay with **you**."

Now, I don't mind saying that I was not only shocked, but more than a little hurt. Not *friends?* **Never** were? After all we'd been through together? And she wanted to stay with Mummy? After all she'd been through with *her?*

"Do you think I forgot about the stunt you pulled?" Mummy said, thumping a finger into the Thief's chest "Stealing my truck was bad enough. But the *silver!*"

"The Brat's silver?" the Know-It-All said to Mummy. "B-b-b-but she left it for you!"

Mummy's face went from furious to puzzled to pleased as she realized something.

"Wait a minute," she said. "She did not *tell* you she took the silver, did she? Which means she did not give it back to you!"

"What," Goody-Two-Shoes said, "what do you mean?"

"She means that before I rescued all of you," the Thief said, "I took the Brat's chest of silver and put it in a secret hiding place."

"I **knew** it!" the Brat said, his face gone blood red and his mouth spitting. "I **knew** I was right about you! You *are* nothing but a dirty rotten thief!"

"What did you expect?" she said. "My name *is* the Thief."

She turned back to Mummy.

"If you were me, you would've done the same thing."

Mummy shrugged. "True."

"Listen, if I tell you where I hid the silver, are we square?" the Thief said. "Will you let me back in the family?"

Mummy smiled. And then put an arm around the Thief.

"Why of course I will, my dear, *dear* daughter!"

And that was it—we wuz betrayed.

By one of our own!

And in case you're thinking things couldn't get any worse, let me tell you:

They did.

There's only one episode left in our tale. You don't want to miss it—it's a DOOZY.

EPISODE SEVEN:
HERE COMES MUMMY CLAUS

---

45. THE NINETY-NINE NIGHTS OF THE NO-GOOD NINE

With the tip of my spearhead, I made another notch on the wall above where I slept. It was so dark, it was hard to make the marks out, so I had to feel at them with my fingers to count—*1, 2, 3, 4, 5, 6, 7, 8, 9*—making tonight *10*. So I slashed a line through all the notches, making it the tenth time I had marked a set, which meant it was

ONE HUNDRED DAYS.

We had been stuck in here for ONE **HUNDRED** DAYS!

"No, we haven't!" the Know-It-All said. "You c-c-c-counted today two times!"

"Did not!" I said. "I made a mark for tonight, and then I counted them, and then I . . . *oooh, right.*"

Geez, I really *did* stink at math.

Let's try that again.

We had been stuck here for NINETY-**NINE** DAYS!

That's still a lot.

If marking off the days on a wall sounds like the kind of thing you do in prison, it's because we *were* in prison.

Elf prison.

"Will you stop whining?" the Cruel said. "It's not even a prison! It's a storeroom. And it's a lot nicer than the orphanage."

How bad *was* that orphanage?

And why did everyone have to keep correcting me?

"I don't wanna *be* here anymore," the Hooligan said, pawing at his lucky rabbit's foot. His eyes were red. "I **hate** this place."

"What are *you* so upset about?" the Brat said. "You were going to wind up in prison anyway. Just like your brother."

The Hooligan's face switched from broken-up to wanting to break something, and he shoved the Brat in the chest. "*What* did you say, bow tie boy?"

"I **said**—"

"Will you all please **SHUT UP!**" the Rude shouted. "Some of us are trying to sleep here." He rolled over in his spot on the floor. "And people say **I'm** rude!"

"You better all be quiet!" came a squeaky voice from outside the door. It was Hendrick, the night guard elf. "You don't want Rooster Jack coming by again!"

"Aw that chump don't bother me," the Hooligan said.

"Well, *you* bother me," the Cruel said.

In case you can't tell, we were getting on each others' nerves. That's what happens when you're forced into hard labor all day and sent to sleep with no dinner in a dismal, near-windowless prison, or storeroom, or whatever you wanted to call it.

As for the hard labor part, we were mostly hauling stuff to the factory. And boy oh *boy*, what a factory.

A lot had happened in the last hundred days.

"N-n-ninety-*nine* days."

Whatever. The point is, Mummy had managed to utterly transform Isle X in the last three months, thanks to her new helpers. You can't believe how these elves could build! It wasn't just toys they could make—they could lay a brick wall, erect steel girders, and slap on a roof faster than my momma could cook Sunday dinner.

Then there was the giant distillery with the great big vats they constructed, not to mention an entirely new assembly line.

This assembly line wasn't for toys, however. It was for bottling.

Huge shiploads of sugar and molasses arrived at Isle X to be boiled, fermented, turned into alcohol, and stored in barrels. From them, each bottle had to be filled, corked, and a label stuck on it. The labels read:

MUMMY'S X-TRA YUMMY
ELF-MADE RUMMY

While the elves did the important work, we Ninesters did the grunt work, taking the booze and putting it into the warehouse, loading the booze from the warehouse onto the sleigh, and unloading the shipments so the elves could make *more* booze. Oh, and that wasn't the worst part. The *worst* part was having to shovel coal into the furnaces and stoking the fires.

The only job I didn't hate was unloading the ship, because that was when I got to talk to Capt. Smudge. I couldn't help but like the guy, despite what he had done. Or was doing.

"How can you *help* Mummy?" I said to him. "Don't you know she's the bad guy?"

His one-word answer:

"Money."

That seemed to be all most adults ever cared about— and the reason the world was such a disaster—but at least it was a reason I could understand. The elves, on the other hand, were helping Mummy for the dumbest reason ever—the suit!

It was like that big red suit hypnotized them. How could anyone take Mummy seriously wearing that stupid thing? Especially with the beard. But even Lefty followed her every order.

Us Naughty Listers, on other hand, broke stuff and messed up whenever we could. But as this kind of sabotage would only land us in solitary confinement (which was in—*yuck*—the old outhouse), we pretty much had begun to toe the line, too. Even the Hooligan, who just *loved* to break stuff.

At the end of every night, we wound up like this—all of us arguing and equally angry.

Actually, that last part's not true. *One* person in the lockup was angrier than the rest of us.

The elf formerly known as Santa Claus.

All his blame and anger, he took out on *us*. Like it was because of *us* that Mummy had come to Isle X!

"Actually, it *was* because of us that Mummy came to Isle X," Goody-Two-Shoes said.

Oh, right.

"Yes, it WAS. And I bet you children are very satisfied with yourselves now," ex-Santa grumbled. "Since all you Naughty Listers ever wanted to do in the first place was RUIN Christmas!"

"We never meant to ruin nuttin'!" the Hooligan said. "We just wanted a little Christmas for ourselves."

"Yeah," the Rude said. "You should blame yourself! If you treated the worker elves better, maybe they wouldn't've all been so quick to work for Mummy."

"You didn't even pay them in real money," the Cruel said. "*Santa* tokens? You were cheating them!"

"And your factory wouldn't have even *gotten* ruined if you had a sprinkler system and a proper fire department!" the Brat said.

"Now, now, don't blame Mr. Santa," the Truant Officer said, just as the elf was rising to defend himself. "It is my fault. I am a trained secret agent, after all. I will never forgive myself for having been taken in by Mrs. Mummy like that."

"It's O.K.," I said. "We *all* got snookered by her." I gave him a pat on the back.

Sometimes even your archenemy needs a little reassuring.

"Well, *I* say—"

Just as the Vainglorious was about to say something sure to make no sense, he was cut off.

"You say nothing. Lights out."

It was the Thief.

She was standing in the doorway, right next to Rooster Jack, with Hendrick behind them.

"Well, if it's not the traitor, come to wish us nighty-night," the Cruel said, glowering.

The Thief gave no response—not to any of us. Rooster Jack said something to her in French, and they left. The Thief slammed the heavy wood door shut behind them

SLAM!

and slid the iron bolt into the jamb

ERRRR!

locking us in.

I could only shake my head.

The Thief—she was the one who *really* snookered us.

46. AND ON THE HUNDREDTH DAY

—**BZZT!**—*Wake up, elves! Wake up, my children! This is your Mummy Claus speaking. Your Mummy 'oo loves you! Your Mummy 'oo only wants the best for you! Now, get OUT of your bunks and get to WORK! My rum doesn't make itself!!*—**BZZT!**—

—**BZZT!**—*That means you too, No-Good Nine!!!*—**BZZT!**—

This was what we woke up to every morning. Lovely, ain't it?

Not that it woke *all* of us up. Some of my fellow Ninesters were still asleep when I heard the *ERRRR!* of the bolt getting thrown back. It was, as usual, Rooster Jack and the Thief.

"Sonnez les matines!" Rooster Jack said, and gave a boot to the snoring Rude.

"Hey!" the Rude said, waking.

Rooster Jack squatted down next to him and sniffed, then held his nose and stuck out his tongue.

"Bleh!"

"You like that? Here, have some more," the Rude

said, flapping his arm like a wing and fanning the smell toward Rooster.

"You all better get going," the Thief said. "There's a new shipment coming in today."

Rooster Jack went to kick the Rude again. "All right, all right, ya goon! I'm gettin' up."

I filed out behind the Cruel, who leaned in and gave a shoulder shove to the Thief as she passed her in the doorway.

"*Sorry*," the Cruel said as unapologetically as possible.

The Cruel was insulting the Thief at every opportunity. Even more than she normally would have.

The Thief, however, never responded. Which was weird—it wasn't like the Thief to take nothing from nobody. But as soon as she got around Mummy and the Brothers Jack, she acted totally different. Maybe it was a family thing, but still it made me wonder. Why did she *really* turn against us?

The Brat wondered no such thing. I think he was actually *glad* the Thief wound up being a traitor, since it meant he had been right about her all along.

(Have you ever noticed how much people like being right?)

As for her criminal family, it turned out that Black Jack and Rooster Jack were orphans like her—or runaways, anyways—and had had the same rotten luck to wind up with Mummy. She'd even named them, too.

Since the ship hadn't arrived yet, I got put on bottle duty. The elf at the end of the assembly line filled up the cases, which it was my job to haul to the storeroom. What I couldn't get was why these elves just did what they were told. It wasn't like they were whistling while they worked. They were all miserable! They were only happy on market day, but even then they could hardly buy anything because they got paid peanuts. *Worse* than peanuts—Santa tokens! It was an outrage. Hadn't they ever heard of going on strike?

I was glad when I heard the horn of Capt. Smudge's ship wailing off in the distance and the loudspeaker crackling for us to go to the docks. While we waited for the ship to pull in, Mummy and the Brothers Jack huddled off to one side.

"S-s-something's different," the Know-It-All said.

"What's different?" the Brat said. "We do the same stupid work every day. Look—I have a callus! No member of my family has *ever* had a callus!"

"Not that," the Know-It-All said. "The w-w-whispering. They never w-w-whisper."

"Who cares?" the Rude said. "It's not like we can understand them anyway."

Which—when you think about it—only made the whispering more strange.

But that wound up not being the only different thing. Normally, Capt. Smudge brought molasses and other raw material for making Mummy's booze. But today we were unloading crates—**heavy** crates—and they were all marked

U.S. ARMY SURPLUS

Mummy also took us into a place to unload them where none of us had ever been before.

The vault.

"Wow, lookit all this loot!" The Rude whistled. The room was packed with money, and more. "Hey, Bratty-boy—ain't that your silver?"

It was. The Brat's chest sat right in the middle of the vault, its top open to reveal the gleaming stacks of silver coins sitting inside.

The Brat's blood started rushing up. Even his *eyes* went red this time.

The Rude was so busy gawking that he bumped into the Vainglorious, who dropped his crate. It smashed open. And there, packed in sawdust, were six machine guns.

We were carrying weapons!

"Oopsie," the Hooligan said, letting his crate drop to the ground. It popped apart, and out bounced sticks of dynamite.

"Be *careful*, you idiots!" Mummy said. "You could blow us all up!"

"*What does she n-n-need all this for?*" the Know-It-All whispered to me on the way out.

I shrugged.

Whatever it was, it wasn't good.

◆ ◆ ◆

The best part of every day was lunch. "Best" because it was our one break from work. Definitely not because of the food, even though it was our only meal of the day.

The problem was that the food was always Mummy's rock-hard horrible biscuits. We gnawed on them while she and her brood ate great big sloppy sandwiches and chips. It was even worse than with Lumiuk's father.

Mummy and the two Jacks were off at their own table while the Thief ate at ours. Whether this was to punish us or her, I'm not sure.

The Thief stared down at her food as she ate, while the Cruel sneered at her.

"*You*," the Cruel said. "You're too ashamed to even look at us. I had it right when I decked you!"

It was actually pretty tame insulting by the Cruel's standards, and—like I said—the Thief never said anything back.

Until now.

The Thief raised her eyes to meet the Cruel's and leaned across the table.

"You think you're so tough? So *cruel*?" the Thief said, giving a sneer of her own. "Your problem is that you're not cruel *enough*."

She stood and looked to each of us in turn.

"It's the problem with *all* of you!" she said. "*The No-Good Nine.* Hah! The Not-So-No-Good Nine is more like it. If any of you knew what it took to survive, you would know that the only person you can trust is *yourself.*"

"That is *not* true!" the Vainglorious said. "We're a team! One for nine, and nine for one!"

"Oh, *please!*" the Thief and the Cruel said in unison.

◆ ◆ ◆

The last task of the day was loading up one of the sleighs with booze.

The sun was already down and there was a crisp chill in the air. Then it started snowing.

In *May.*

We **had** to get out of here.

The deliveries had started weeks ago, as soon as the bottles began coming off the assembly line. Mummy would fly to her old buyers, land on their roofs, and deliver the rum down their chimneys. At first, she delivered only a few cases, but every night it was more.

While Rooster stayed to keep an eye on Isle X, Black

Jack drove the sleigh, a skill he had learned from Driver Elf.

Not that he had learned too good. It seemed like Black Jack's only technique was to beat the reindeer with a whip.

"I'd like to beat *him* with a whip," Goody-Two-Shoes said.

(Even Goody could get violent when innocent animals were involved.)

Normally, this was when Mummy was in her best mood, but today she was preoccupied. She didn't even cackle her usual *"AH-AH-AH!"*s.

What *was* going on?

As soon as the sleigh was packed, Mummy blasted her air horn—**BLANNNNH!**—and Black Jack cracked the whip. In an instant, they were up and off, flying southward against the silhouette of the moon.

It would've been beautiful, if it hadn't've been so horrible.

◆ ◆ ◆

Even though I had already done it yesterday, I redrew the slash to mark the set of ten.

One HUNDRED days. For real.

Hooray.

How many *more* hundreds of days would we be stuck here?

I told you how one of us was even angrier and more

miserable than the rest of us to be in the lockup. There was also a Ninester who wasn't angry or miserable at all.

"Prison sweet prison!" the Vainglorious said. "It's not really so terrible, is it, fellers? After all, at least we've got each other!"

Everyone pounced on the poor guy. Me, I was so exhausted, I just fell asleep to the sound of the arguing. I was used to it.

Now, this *should* be where this really long chapter finally ends, but it's not. Because that thing that kept happening happened *again*.

We woke up to someone surprising us.

But this someone wasn't lurking or sneaking.

They were barging in. **Loudly.**

"Wake up! Wake up, my children! Merry Christmas! MERRRRRY Christmas!"

I had to rub my eyes, because for a minute, I thought it really *was* Santa Claus, what with the red suit and hat and the stuffed sack slung across their back.

Of course, the *real* Santa was lying on the floor next to me in his dirty underwear, snoring. And when *this* Santa reached into the bag, she pulled out wads of money to toss into the air.

"Merry Christmas! *AH-AH-AH!*" Mummy cackled.

I plucked one of the fluttering notes out of the air. It was a hundred-dollar bill! Now I *really* thought I was dreaming.

"'Ere, my children, take the money! Take this 'ole sack! And you want to know why?" Mummy said. "Because if not for YOU, none of this would 'ave 'appened to me!"

Mummy pulled her beard below her chin and flipped it around so it hung down the back of her suit like a furry white cape. With her teeth, she pulled the cork out of one of her bottles of elf-made rum and held it high.

"Tonight I toast to you, my children. And to ME!"

She took a swig.

"Do you know 'oo I met tonight? You will never believe it," she said. "Al CAPONE!" She took off the hat when she said it, like the very name demanded respect.

"And 'e 'as 'eard of *me*—of Mummy Rummy! Can you imagine? Al Capone 'imself!"

She pressed the hat to her heart.

"What is more, 'e wants to do business with me. The entire Syndicate does! Tonight, they placed the biggest order of booze any rumrunner 'as ever 'AD!"

She took another drink and—instead of cackling—laughed a smaller, more self-satisfied kind of laugh.

"'E thinks I will work for 'im—they all do, *ah-ah-ah*," she said. "But soon they will be working for **me**!"

"Is that what all the weapons are for?" Goody-Two-Shoes said. "To take over the *Mob*?"

"Those guns are for protection!" Mummy said, grinning. "In case some other bootlegger gets wise to my operation and tries to take it over. I am going to turn Isle X into a fortress, children. Other bootleggers can 'ave Canada. I will 'ave my own *country*! With an elf army to defend it!"

"You're going to make the elves use *guns?*" the Truant Officer said, 'orrified. I mean, *hor*rified.

"Why, of course!" Mummy said. "But first, we 'ave an order to fill. The factory must be going day and night! Three days—we only 'ave THREE DAYS! And then it will be Christmas for Mummy!"

She took one more swig.

"But then, *every* day will be Christmas for Mummy! *AH-AH-AH!!!*"

It was your classic bad-guy gloating session. This was a part of hero-ing I'd come to expect later. Y'see, it's no fun for a bad guy to do all their badness unless they can brag about it to someone else, preferably the one person (or *group* of persons) who could stop them but is otherwise trapped. They save their biggest brag for the moment when they are on the brink of total victory. In the movies, it never works out for the bad guy. But we weren't in no movie.

"Now, no going back to sleep!" Mummy said. "Get up and get to *work!*"

She left, still swigging and cackling.

"Would the elves *really* do that?" Goody asked Santa. "Shoot guns?"

Santa shrugged. "She wears the suit."

Me, I could not believe it.

I had a *hundred bucks!*

I looked down at the crisp green bill.

"Don't be so h-h-happy," the Know-It-All said. "It's only a piece of paper if you don't have anything to b-b-buy with it."

He really should have been called the Killjoy.

"We have to stop her," the Truant Officer said.

"Stop her?" the Hooligan said. "We can't stop her! Al Capone can't even stop her! All *I* want is some real food!"

"I'd take not having to sleep on this freezing stone floor," the Rude said.

"I just want to l-l-l-leave!" the Know-It-All said.

"Well, none of what *any* of you want is going to happen," the Cruel said. "So we might as well get up and go to work."

"You're wrong," I said. "One thing we want *is* going to happen. We're going to leave. In three days! And I know just how we're going to do it."

And that was no lie.

47. A REALLY SHORT CHAPTER IN WHICH A SWELL PLAN IS AGREED TO

The most amazing part of my escape plan was that everyone not only listened to me, they agreed to *do* it.

Which, frankly, should tell you more about the quality of our options than how much faith my fellow No-Good Ninesters had in me.

But the thing was, in order to escape from a prison like this, you had to have a plan that was tricky and deceitful.

Once again, this was *my* department.

My plan would swing into action right after Mummy left to make her big delivery. Because I know you're anxious, let's just skip all the boring talking and get to that part—the *good* part—right now!

48. A FAKE FRACAS

"Keep *loading*! I don't care 'ow 'eavy it is," Mummy barked. "On the way back, the sleigh will be much lighter! Money does weigh less than liquor! *AH-AH-AH!*"

Mummy was giddy, but you can sure bet no one else was. Because she hadn't been joking when she said she'd keep the factory going day and night. I'm not sure how the elves managed to stay on their feet so long. Of course, *they* were no longer on their feet. They had trudged off to the elf barracks and were probably already asleep in their bunks, while *we* still had to pack this stupid sleigh.

And it wasn't one of those speedy little models like we had been loading. No, tonight we were packing the industrial-strength sleigh—THE XMAS NITE SPECIAL. The thing was so huge, it took eight reindeer to pull instead of the usual one or two.

As we loaded the last of the cases onto the sleigh, Mummy took her place on the seat next to Black Jack.

"Don't wait up, children! I might not be back for days!" she said. "And when I *do* come back, I will be the Queen of the Mob! *AH-AH-AH!*"

That evil laugh was really getting annoying. But it wasn't as bad as the

BLAAAANH!

of the air horn Mummy blasted as the sleigh lifted off the ground—barely—and flew up into the sky.

As Rooster Jack and the Thief led us away for the night, the Truant Officer spoke up loudly.

"Just another NORMAL night of walking home to our prison," he said.

How was this guy *ever* a spy? He was going to blow our whole scheme before we even started!

Luckily, Rooster Jack and the Thief weren't paying any attention. However, as she was about to bar the door, the Thief *did* notice something was off.

She cocked her head to one side and looked at the Cruel. "What, no insult tonight?" she said.

The Cruel rolled her eyes.

"The fun is gone," she said.

The Thief's face twisted into a skeptical knot as she slammed the door shut and bolted it

SLAM! ERRR!

Now the only person watching us was Hendrick, the night guard elf.

As far as guards go, Hendrick was pretty bad. For one thing, he was too nice; for another, he always fell asleep. Of course, with only one tiny barred window and a bolted front door a foot thick, there wasn't much chance of us escaping.

Not unless Hendrick *let* us out.

It was time for the plan to begin!

"Get outta my way," the Rude said to me.

"No, you get outta *my* way!" I said, loud enough that Hendrick could hear. "I am so tired of you being such a rude little jerk!"

(Which *was* true.)

At this point, the Rude raised a finger at me—I think you know the one—and said, "Climb it, Tarzan!"

"*Ooooh!*" the other Ninesters went.

It was hard to tell which of us threw the first punch, because we did it at pretty much the same time.

Then we started pounding each other, not so much because it was a part of the plan as it was just plain fun.

"Hey! Why don't you two fellers break it up, will you?" the Truant Officer said in the worst fake voice imaginable.

I groaned.

My nemesis was *really* awful at this.

"Come on, you are all friends here!" he said.

"I'm *not* his friend!" I said.

"Me **neither**!" the Rude said.

We fell into a heap on the floor and started rolling around, wrestling.

"Is it working?" I whispered. *"Is Hendrick buying it?"*

The Know-It-All, looking out the little window, shook his head no.

"You should just stop fighting," Goody-Two-Shoes said.

"Ah, let them fight!" the Cruel said. "It's fun watching these two beat each other's brains in."

"You know who *I* want to fight?" Goody said. "You!"

"Oh, Goody-*Two*-Shoes wants to fight, does she?" the Cruel said. "This is gonna be—*oof*!"

The Cruel couldn't finish the sentence because Goody had tackled her in the gut.

"Katie-bar-the-door, it's a brawl!" the Hooligan said. "I want in on this!"

He head-butted the Brat, and now *everyone* was at it.

"Will you cretins stop this nonsense!" Santa said as we wrestled each other. "I should make a Stupid List and put you all at the top of it! Can't you see your plan is NOT WORKING!"

We all stopped except for the Vainglorious, who—as usual—wasn't listening. He landed a punch right to the face of the Rude, who had let his guard down. For the first time, I saw the the shortest Ninester get *mad*.

"Sorry?" the Vainglorious said.

If you thought the Rude wasn't tough because he was small, you'd be wrong. He didn't work at a boxing gym for nothing.

He gave the Vainglorious a couple of lightning-quick jabs to the face and then

POW!

landed a right cross to his solar plexus.

It looked like it hurt. A *lot*.

The Vainglorious doubled over

"OOF!"

and his open mouth—which is to say his *teeth*—landed right in the Rude's skull.

There was a whole lot of bleeding. The Rude from the top of his head, the Vainglorious from his mouth.

There was a whole lot of wailing in pain, too.

"What's going on in there?" Hendrick finally asked from the other side of the door.

"They got hurt! They're bleeding real bad!" I yelled. "You have to let us out!"

"I'll call the ambulance!" Hendrick hollered. "I'll get Dr. Elf!"

"There's no time for that!" I said. "You have to come in here—we need to take them NOW!"

I heard the sweet *errr!* of the bolt getting thrown back. Hendrick's face went pale when he saw the blood, and he rushed to check on the Rude and the Vainglorious.

"You poor children!" he said. "Don't worry! Dr. Elf will help!"

Then Hendrick turned back and saw all of us looking down at him.

"Uh-oh," he said.

◆ ◆ ◆

We should have been racing outside to hop aboard a sleigh—that was the next part of the plan—but Goody-Two-Shoes insisted on playing nurse again.

"I might have to stitch that up," she said, looking at the top of the Rude's head.

"No! Please no!" the Rude said. "I saw what you did to the Cruel! You ain't puttin' no needle through my scalp!"

While the Rude begged for mercy, I went to look at the Vainglorious's mouth.

I told him to smile. It was not pretty.

His teeth were outlined in blood, which was bad enough, but the *really* gross thing was that one of his front teeth was askew. In fact, it was practically sideways.

"Is it bad?" the Vainglorious asked.

"No," I said. "Not at all."

And that's when the tooth fell out and dropped to the stone floor with a bounce.

The Vainglorious picked it up, and for some reason seemed pleased.

The Know-It-All asked why he wasn't more upset.

The Vainglorious shrugged. "It'll grow back."

"*What* will grow back?" the Know-It-All asked.

"The tooth."

"No, it won't!"

"Sure it will," the Vainglorious said. "I've lost every single tooth in my head, and they've *all* grown back. And the Tooth Fairy always leaves me something. Unlike *Santa*."

Santa rolled his eyes.

"But those were your baby—"

"Don't say another word, Know-It-All!" I said. I turned to the Vainglorious. "He's just teasing, pal. The tooth'll grow back. *Sure* it'll grow back. You put that under your pillow, and the Tooth Fairy will bring you sump'm *real* nice!"

Now it was time for the next part of our plan.

And that's when things got all mucked up.

From the open door came a sudden stream of loud and menacing threats. Exactly what was said, I can't tell you, because it was said in French.

Rooster Jack!

He had a gun. Pointed right at *me*.

Well, it was pointed at all of us, but it *felt* like it was pointed right at me.

Anyway, we put our hands up but he kept yelling and I thought he was gonna shoot and then

BLAM!

The sound was *not* from a gun.

It was from a bat. To the back of Rooster Jack's head.

Mummy's sonny-boy went down with a

THUD!

revealing who had done the swinging.

The Thief!

She tossed her weapon to the ground.

"It's me, stupid," she said.

I did love that password.

49. BUT SHOULD WE BELIEVE HER?

It was weird. We were all just standing around looking at the Thief, silently. A cold wind whistled in through the open door behind her, Rooster Jack lay unconscious on the floor before her, and you're probably thinking the same thing I was.

Haven't we *been* through this before?

When we first met her, the Thief helped us. Then she betrayed us and stole the Brat's money. *Then* she saved us. *Then* she betrayed us—again. And now she had saved us—*again*!

"Cantcha just make up yer mind *which* side you're on?" the Hooligan said.

The Thief looked at him like she couldn't believe what he was saying.

"I'm on *your* side," she said. "I've only been pretending to be with Mummy!"

Now the Cruel was the one looking like she couldn't believe what she was hearing.

"*Puh!*" she spit out. "Why on earth should we believe **you**?"

"Because I am *helping* you escape! Look," the Thief said, pointing. "The door is wide open. Mummy is *gone*. All you have to do is take one of her sleighs and you're free! None of us could have escaped if I was trapped inside here, too."

It was a good point, you have to admit.

"Well, I still don't believe her!" the Brat said, a ripe red tantrum rising into his face. "It's some kind of **trick**!"

"*What* trick? Do you think I want to get in trouble with Mummy again?" the Thief said. "Look, we have to hurry. We only have a few hours to break into Mummy's safe and take her money and get out of here!"

"Wait," the Know-It-All said. "The p-p-p-plan is to *leave*! I don't want to get c-c-caught trying to steal her money."

"No, hold on. She *does* have the right idea," the Brat said, his greed overriding his tantrum. "I may not trust her, but we should definitely take the money. And my silver is in there, too!"

Take the money and run, or *just* run? There was a whole lot of arguing over which tack to take, but Goody-Two-Shoes wasn't having either of them.

"What about Christmas? What about *Mummy*?" she said. Not only had we ruined the holiday, Goody pointed out, we'd given Mummy access to a magical manufacturing empire. "Didn't you guys hear what she's planning? She's going to take over the Mob, and it's *our* fault. We have to **stop** her!"

Believe it or not, the first No-Good Ninester to step forward and take a stand alongside Goody was the Cruel.

Her reason for wanting to stay and stop Mummy, however, had nothing to do with making amends or anything noble like that.

"I want revenge on that miserable bootlegger," the Cruel said.

The Brat seconded the notion. My archenemy however, saw things differently.

"Revenge helps no one," the Truant Officer said. "But this woman does need to be stopped."

"Let's start by smashing up the factory," the Hooligan said. "I *hate* that place."

"Yeah!" the Rude said. "We did such a good job of

wrecking it by mistake, think of how great we'll do when it's on purpose!"

There were more excited shouts, and everyone was getting all riled and ready to have at it. With the exception of *one* naysayer.

"If you think you can stop Mummy, then all you Naughty Listers are even DUMBER than I thought," Santa said. "She has the *elves*. Even if you managed to get her money and destroy the factory *and* escape, the elves would just rebuild it and she'd make even more money! And imagine what she'd do to you if she CAUGHT you?" Santa smiled at the thought of it. Then harrumphed. "You should all just leave—while you still can!"

Everyone began arguing over what to do. It was chaos, and time was running out.

If someone was going to save the situation—to bring us together in one common purpose—it was going to have to be me.

Yeah, that's right. *Me*.

I stuck my fingers in my mouth and gave the loudest whistle I could. Everyone stopped yelling and stared in my direction.

I began by reminding my fellow members of why we had banded together in the first place.

"Remember, if the No-Good Nine stands for anything, it's about doing whatever we want. So let's take the money—*and* smash the factory—*and* escape this island—*and* stop Mummy, too! Because Goody-Two-Shoes and my archenemy are right. We can't just ruin Christmas and let Mummy run the Mob. This is *our* fault and *we* have to stop it!"

It was a swell speech if I do say so myself, but I didn't mean any of it. Stopping Mummy didn't matter much to me, and what did I care about fixing Christmas? It wasn't like *I'd* be getting any presents, and was Mummy really going to be a worse mob boss than *Al Capone*?

No, what I couldn't bear was the thought of all those elves following a dumb red suit. We had to show them they could think for themselves!

"But *how*?" the Know-It-All said. "You h-h-heard what Santa said."

"Don't worry," I said. "I have a plan."

"Oh yeah? And how did your *last* plan turn out?" the Cruel said. "If not for the Thief making like Babe Ruth with Rooster Jack's head, we'd still be trapped in here, or worse!"

"Yeah, but this is a *good* plan," I said.

I smiled.

No one else looked convinced.

"One for nine?" I said, making the Sign of the Nine across my chest.

Everyone shrugged and gave a very unenthusiastic, "Nine for one . . ."

The Truant Officer was in, too. And so was Hendrick,

who never much cared for Mummy Claus.

Just as I was about to explain *how* we were going to break the elves away from Mummy's control, the Hooligan raised his hand.

"Does any of this plannin' stuff involve us gettin' sump'm to eat?"

50. THE BEST CHAPTER YET!

Getting food was the easy part. With Rooster Jack tied up, gagged, and locked in our old prison, we were able to stroll into Santa's former house and pull a rack of meat out of the fridge.

"Take off your boots!" Santa said. "And get your *feet* off the table!"

"This ain't your house no more, remember?" the Rude said, and wiped his mouth on the tablecloth.

As we filled our bellies, I revealed the Plan.

"I call it . . . The GREAT ELF UPRISING!"

The name was aces, right?

First, we'd split into four groups, each designed to take advantage of the special—er—*talents* of its members.

The first team was the least likely, as it put the Thief and the Brat together. The reason for this was that the Brat didn't trust the Thief with what she was going to do.

Namely, break into Mummy's vault and steal all her loot, which included *his* loot. (We'd be doing something else with Mummy's arsenal of weapons. More on that later.)

The members of group two—the Hooligan, the Rude, and Hendrick the guard elf—would be on factory-wrecking duty.

Team three would make use of Goody-Two-Shoes's particular brand of naughtiness. To help her were the Cruel, the Vainglorious, and a very special friend. More on *him* later.

Because first I have to tell you about the final—and most important—squad, which was made up of the Know-It-All, Santa, the Truant Officer, and myself.

We would be delivering the morning message, and it would be a message unlike any the elves had ever heard before.

"But how is it going to change their minds?" Santa said.

A fair question. This speech was going to have to be so amazing—incredible—indisputable that the elves would have no *choice* but to believe it.

"And *you* are going to read it!" I told Santa. He harrumphed and crossed his arms.

While the others left to carry out their assignments, the Know-It-All and I stayed to write the irresistible speech.

It took us a couple of hours, but when you combined the Know-It-All's sense of reason and smarts with my own sense of drama and deceit, it led to something pretty darn good.

"I can't read THIS!" Santa said as he looked it over. "I don't believe a word of it!"

"But you've gotta read it!" I said. "It's the only way to convince the other elves not to follow the suit. And besides, don't you *want* to be Santa again?"

He threw the script to the ground.

"Santa, I think you had better start believing it," the Truant Officer said, reaching for the dropped paper. "*Every* word of it."

My archenemy held the speech out for Santa to take.

"YOU are telling me this?" Santa said. "You are the one who crossed five thousand miles of subarctic wilderness to stop these dirty rotten Naughty Listers! What about them being a bunch of spoiled American *negodniks*?"

"I was wrong, Santa. And so are you," my nemesis said. Then he turned to me. "I was especially wrong about *you*, Luigi Curidi."

Oh, yuck! How could he say that to me? Was my archenemy going all soft on me now? Were we going to have to become *friends* or something?

Under any other circumstances, I would've told him to go to heck—we were nemesisses and that was that.

However, with enemies like Mummy and Black Jack, I needed all the friends I could get.

"Just never call me that name again, O.K.?"

◆ ◆ ◆

When we stepped out of Santa's house, the sky was just beginning to brighten in the east, drowning out the stars on the horizon. While the rest of my group went to the Eye to get the morning broadcast ready, I went to check on the progress of the other teams. First, I stopped by the factory.

Walking in, I almost got brained by a case of flying bottles.

"Hey, watch where you're goin'!" the Rude said, glass shattering everywhere. "We're destroyin' stuff here!"

It looked like an earthquake had hit the joint. The equipment was smashed—the Hooligan and Hendrick were swinging sledgehammers at everything in sight—and the floor was covered in shards of glass, sticky puddles of molasses, and a murky river of ruined rum.

"Great job, fellers!" I said.

"Thanks," the Rude said. "Now help me roll these barrels."

"Uh, I actually have to go check on the others," I said.

Physical labor was *not* my talent.

Inside Mummy's vault, I found the Brat and the Thief having—what else?—an argument.

"I stole it fair and square!" the Thief said, pulling the trunk of silver away from the Brat. "It's *mine!*"

"But it was mine *first!*" the Brat said, yanking on the opposite handle.

"No, it wasn't," she said. "It was your *daddy's*. And he stole it from someone **else**!"

The Brat looked like his head was about to pop off.

"Guys, guys!" I said. "Stop it! You were supposed to be carting off the money and the weapons."

The Thief told me that the cash was already loaded into the sleigh, but we had to hurry with Mummy's arsenal. The sun was nearly up!

The three of us pushed wheelbarrows of guns, ammunition, and dynamite down the hill and into the Square, where we found Goody-Two-Shoes's team. They were at work on the walls of the buildings lining the plaza.

And what they had painted on them was fantastic.

Graffiti might have been Goody-Two-Shoes's special skill, but the Cruel and the Vainglorious had the knack for it, too. As did their special helper—Lefty.

"He didn't want to do it at first," Goody said, motioning to the paint-splattered elf. "But he's really taken to it."

"You know that we elves hate to break the rules. But this is **fun**!" Lefty said, finishing up a note to his fellow workers.

I'd tell you what it was, but just then the sun broke the horizon and

*—**BZZT!**—Good morning, fellow elves! This is your Santa speaking. Your FORMER Santa, that is . . .—*

As he read the address, elves began to come out of their sleeping quarters, to better hear what Santa was saying. They were mesmerized, unable to believe his words. Which is to say, *our* words.

It was a beautiful speech, if I do say so myself.

It was about fairness. And justice. And the *true* meaning of Christmas.

"It makes me want to vomit," the Cruel said.

"*Shhh!*" I said. "He's getting to the good part!"

—but more than that, my fellow elves, I want to apologize to all of YOU. I have been wrong about many things. I should have treated you better. I should have paid you more. I should not have worked you so hard. I promise that all this will change if you make me your Santa again. And so will . . . (wait, do I HAVE to say this part?)—

That last bit was muffled, like Santa was covering the microphone.

(. . . but it doesn't even have anything to do with the elves—what do THEY care about the Naughty List?)

The Truant Officer said something garbled in the background, and Santa sighed.

He continued:

—And SO will how we decide who gets presents. Because . . . ahem . . . EVERY child should get presents on Christmas, no matter how ROTTEN or THIEVING or LYING or—

Hey, *that* wasn't in the script!

—or HORRIBLE or WRETCHED they are. And so I announce that—if you DO make me your Santa again—there shall be NO . . . MORE . . . NAUGHTY LIST.—

Bingo!

If you can believe it, even the Cruel gave me a smile and a pat on the back.

O.K., there was no pat. And she didn't smile so much as she just stopped scowling for a moment.

*—In closing, I want to leave you with one last thing that I have learned, and I hope you have too: It is not the suit that makes the Santa, but the SANTA that makes the suit. The only thing any of you should follow is your own mind and, most especially, your own heart. Thank you for listening . . .—***BZZT!**

By the time the broadcast was finished, all the elves had spilled out into the Square, where they stood staring up at the giant loudspeaker attached to the Tower. I waited for them to cheer. It was a most cheer-worthy speech, after all.

But they weren't cheering.

They *still* looked confused.

And that's when we heard

BLANNNNH!

It was the sound of Mummy's sleigh, returning.

Why was she back so early?

I suddenly wondered if we had really thought this thing through.

Whose dumb plan was this anyway?

51. THE RETURN OF MUMMY CLAUS

You almost had to feel bad for Mummy. I mean, imagine—you're coming back from the greatest night of your life, when you not only make a fortune but you impress the most vile and dangerous criminals on the planet so much that they make you a member of their exclusive underworld syndicate. Then you come flying home, thinking of all the glorious bad-guy gloating you're about to get to do, and you see all the elves wandering around the Square, and you know *something* has gone wrong.

So you can see why she was annoyed from the moment she stepped out of that oversize sleigh.

With Black Jack trailing behind her, she walked from the stables toward the Square, where she found a group of elves gathered around a wall.

"What are you fools looking at?" she said.

"*Mummy Rummy is an evil dummy*," one of them said.

"*What* did you just say?" Mummy said, her gold tooth glaring as she snarled.

The elf pointed at the wall.

MUMMY RUMMY IS AN EVIL DUMMY

And that's when Mummy saw it—the graffiti on all the buildings.

DON'T FOLLOW A SUIT

GIVE MUMMY THE BOOT!!
MAKE TOYS NOT BOOZE
THE FREE REPUBLIC OF ELVES!
WORKER ELVES UNITE!

GET NAUGHTY!

NEVER TRUST A LADY WITH A FAKE
BEARD AND A GOLD TOOTH!

DOWN WITH MUMMY!
DOWN WITH MUMMY!
DOWN WITH MUMMY!
DOWN WITH MUMMY!
DOWN WITH MUMMY!

and

THE GLORIOUS IS HANDSOME!

"I can't believe you wrote that!" I said to the Vain-glorious.

"Why do you think it was me?" he said. "*Anyone* could have written that!"

The other teams were now coming to see what was going on, and all nine of us were together again. For the first time.

I flashed the Sign of the Nine. And everyone flashed it back.

Which is when Mummy saw us.

"*The No-Good Nine!*" she said, spitting the words out. "'Ow did you all escape? What did you do to Rooster Jack?"

"He's tied up at the moment," the Thief said.

"*You!*" Mummy said. "I should 'ave known! I never should 'ave trusted you. It is the love a mother 'as for a daughter that leads to such mistakes!"

"And here I thought it was the chest of silver," the Thief said.

"Your factory is destroyed, Mummy," the Rude said. "All of it!"

Her face went white.

"And this is yer last bottle of booze!" the Hooligan said, proudly holding it up.

"That factory was *nothing*!" Mummy said, recovering. "With all the money I've made, I'll build a factory that puts that one to shame. In fact, I'll build *ten* of them. And my army of elves will 'elp me!"

"Yeah, the money—we took all that," the Brat said.

"And the weapons," the Thief said. "They're over there."

She pointed to the big pile in the middle of the Square. Then she nodded to the Hooligan and the Rude.

"Boys?" the Thief said. "Do it!"

The Hooligan pulled the cork out of the bottle of rum with his teeth

Pop!

turned it upside down, and made a trail of alcohol to the pile of weapons. The Rude lit a match, dropped it on the rum, and

FWOOM!

and then

KABOOM!

The fireworks display might have been a bit more intense than we had planned for, but it did the trick.

"*Noooo!*" Mummy shouted. "All my guns! And dynamite! What 'ave you DONE?"

"Ain't it beautiful?" the Rude said.

"You're through, Mummy!" I said. "That was your entire arsenal. All of your guns are gone!"

"Except for these!" she said as she and Black Jack each pulled out a pistol.

Oh, right! I forgot they always carried guns.

"I'll get you for this!" Mummy said, waving her gun at us. "All of you!"

"No, you won't!"

It wasn't one of us who said it. It was an elf.

Amanuensis.

He was at the head of what had become a mob. The elves were headed straight for Mummy, and they no longer looked confused.

"What's the matter with you, you stupid little gnomes!" Mummy said. "Get away from me and get to **WORK**!"

"We're not *going* to work today," Amanuensis said. "Not for **you**."

Mummy's face bubbled with fury.

"**What** did you say?" she said.

"I said," Amanuensis said, "we're not going to work for you. Ever!"

"Don't you see this?" she said, tugging on her red jacket. "And *this*?" She tugged on her beard. "You 'ave to follow me! I wear the suit. I am the Santa!"

"No we don't, and no you're not," Amanuensis said. "You're not an elf, and you're barely even a human being."

He stepped up to Mummy, grabbed the end of the beard, and yanked it off of her

snap!

"'Ow dare you, you little troll!" she said. "Do you 'ave any idea what I can do to you. Why I—I—"

Mummy stopped.

There must've been two hundred elves gathered around her now, and they were closing in.

They did *not* look happy.

Remember what I said about elves holding a grudge? I wasn't kidding.

"You've stolen our home!" an elf shouted from the back of the crowd.

"We don't want to make your rum anymore!" another yelled.

"MAKE TOYS NOT BOOZE!" someone hollered.

There was booing and hissing. And then the chant began.

"DOWN WITH MUMMY! DOWN WITH MUMMY!"

A snowball hit her in the head, knocking the red Santa hat off.

"You worthless *trolls*!" Mummy tried to shout over them. "Fine! See what I care! I've still got enough money from one night to last me a lifetime! You can 'ave your godforsaken freezing rock of an island!!"

Black Jack was backing up slowly, and now Mummy was too.

And then they made a run for it.

Snowballs went flying after them. One nailed Mummy right in the keister. Which is to say, her big red butt.

The elves all cheered, and so did we.

But just as I was getting ready to celebrate our hard-earned happy ending, the Truant Officer grabbed me.

"We can't let Mummy escape!" he yelled above the commotion. "We have to go after her and Black Jack!"

Was he serious? Did he not *see* the guns? Didn't he realize that we only have one chapter left?

"Come on!" he said, and raced off after them.

I sighed. And then I started running too.

This was the problem with archenemies. They spoiled *everything*.

52. THE FLYING SLEIGH RACE

I had never seen Mummy run before, and it wasn't pretty. It was less running and more like waddling quickly.

Needless to say, my archenemy and I were able to beat her to the sleigh. She had parked the XMAS NITE SPECIAL right outside the stable, with the reindeer still hitched to it.

"So, what's our plan?" I asked my nemesis.

"We tell them to stop."

"We *tell* them to stop?" I said.

This was a terrible plan!

"Stop! In the name of the Sewickley Department of Attendance!" the Truant Officer hollered, holding up his stupid tin badge.

Mummy and Black Jack were *not* stopping.

I had to hide! But where?

I hopped into the sleigh, but the whole huge thing was stuffed full with bulging sacks of cash. I found a half-empty one and wriggled myself inside.

As I did, the Truant Officer rushed Black Jack and grabbed his pistol arm.

BLAM!

A stray bullet went shooting up into the air as the two of them grappled.

Meanwhile, Mummy took the opportunity to get into the sleigh.

Where I was hiding!

"Mush, you flea-bitten beasts!" I heard Mummy say, followed by the

CRACK

of the whip.

I got a real queasy feeling in my stomach, like I was on a roller coaster.

Were we . . . *flying?*

"Mummy!" Black Jack said. "Wait for me!"

(At least, that's what I'm guessing he said. I don't speak French, remember?)

"Take one of the other sleighs, you idiot!" she hollered, pointing to the stables.

As I was, at that point, stuffed inside a sack—flying higher and (*gulp!*) higher—I really didn't know what was going on with Black Jack after that. But I'm not going to let that stop me from telling you exactly what happened.

Because Black Jack did head over to get another sleigh at the stables, where he found the Hooligan, the Rude, and the Thief waiting for him. As for how those three got there and what happened to the rest of the No-Good Nine, well, I can't tell you right now because

BLAM!

He shot at them!

BLAM BLAM BLAM!

Amazingly—foolishly—heroically, the Hooligan hurled himself into the line of fire to protect the Rude and the Thief.

"Hoolie, **NO!**" the Rude shouted.

The Hooligan went down on the ground in a heap, and Black Jack fast hitched a reindeer to a sleigh and took off flying.

The Thief and the Rude rushed to the side of the Hooligan, lying in the straw and manure.

"Ow, my head," he said. "I hit it on the post!"

"How did you not get *shot*?" the Rude said. "He was only five feet away from you when he fired!"

The Hooligan smiled as he showed them what he was holding.

"My lucky rabbit's foot!"

Yeah, some luck that bunny paw had given us for the *last* couple of hundred pages!

In a flash, the Rude had a sleigh and reindeer ready to go, the Thief and the Hooligan climbed aboard, and the chase was ON!

Now I didn't know any of this at the time, because I was still in the sack, praying Mummy wouldn't notice me. Of course, she was plenty preoccupied trying to figure out how to drive the sleigh. It wasn't going well. Or smoothly.

"Black Jack!" she hollered as he came alongside. "'Ow do you steer this thing?!"

"Give it up, Mummy—you're through!" the Rude hollered, having caught up to both our sleigh and Black Jack's.

BLAM BLAM!

Mummy shot at them.

For the record it is *not* a good idea to shoot pistols from the back of a flying sleigh pulled by magical reindeer, magical reindeer not being used to the sound of gunfire.

In fact, it spooked them so bad that they suddenly stopped flying and we

DROPPED

about fifty feet down in the sky.

Ugh, my stomach!

The sleigh pitched sideways, and I got spit out of the sack.

I was suddenly on the floor of the sleigh, in a swirling pile of cash, looking up at Mummy.

"Uh, hi?" I said, and gave her a little wave.

"**You!**" she shouted. "Get out of my money and drive this *tabarnouche* sled!"

"But I don't know how to!"

"Just do it!"

It's amazing how persuasive a person can be when they have a pistol pointed right between your eyes.

I grabbed the reins, but how *was* I supposed to steer this thing? I looked over to the other sleighs for pointers.

The Rude and company were now making a beeline for Black Jack's sleigh. The dirty goon pointed his gun at them, and

BUMP!

The Rude banged his sleigh into Black Jack's, knocking the bad guy off balance and the gun out of his hands. The weapon went plummeting. At the same moment, the Hooligan hopped from one sleigh to the other, tackled Black Jack, and proceeded to beat the tar out of him.

I'm sure glad that kid was on *our* side.

In the meantime, our sleigh pulled ahead.

"Hurry up and get them!" the Thief yelled to the Rude.

I tried to sabotage our ride to make it easier for them to catch us, but everything I did to slow the reindeer down—like pulling back on the reins—only sped them up.

The Rude's sleigh wasn't gaining on us any and the Hooligan was way behind. He was still too busy beating up Black Jack.

"We'll never catch them!" the Thief shouted. "They're too far ahead!"

"Don't worry, we'll catch 'em!" the Rude said.

He dropped the reins and climbed out of the sleigh onto the back of the reindeer. It was just like riding a horse at the track!

Except for the flying part.

"Come on behind me!" he called to the Thief.

The Thief paused, and I could see her gulp all the way from where I was. But she screwed up her courage and hopped on too.

As soon as she was seated behind the Rude, he told her to hold onto his legs.

"What? Why?" she said.

"Just do it!" he said, and flipped himself upside down under the reindeer's belly. From there, he unhitched its harness, and the sleigh went plummeting into the sea.

Free of having to pull the vehicle, the reindeer flew like lightning, with the Rude and the Thief riding on its back.

"Ya-**hoo**!" the Rude hollered as they fast caught up to us and went soaring over our heads.

"What are they *doing*?" Mummy shouted.

I looked up as the air-galloping hooves of the reindeer passed right over our heads. Then I saw the soles of a pair of feet.

It was the Thief! She had leapt *off* the back of the reindeer—

Is she NUTS?—

and landed right in our sleigh.

Unfortunately, she touched down a little to one side, which caused the entire thing to turn sideways. It was only for a moment, but it was long enough to knock me *out* of the sleigh.

"AAAAAH!" I screamed.

I don't know how I did it, but I managed to grab onto one of the runners that were attached to the underside of the sleigh. Try as I might, however, there was no way I could make it back up into the sleigh, and I hung there dangling. I looked down.

Bad idea.

It was *miles* to the ground. Except there was no ground—just open ocean as far as the eye could see!

Meanwhile, the Thief and Mummy were duking it out.

"This is for you, mummy dearest!" the Thief said, and

POW!

landed a fist to her jaw.

"Bad idea, daughter!" Mummy said, and came back up with a

PUNCH!

to the Thief's gut.

"Mother versus daughter!" Mummy said. "Just like it always should be!"

"You are *not* my mother!" the Thief said, cocking a fist. "And I am *not* your daughter!"

The Thief threw a real haymaker, but she missed and spun around on herself. Before she could recover, Mummy was on top of her, both hands around her throat, choking her.

"I am going to kill you like I should 'ave done before!" she said, flashing a big gold-toothed smile.

I could see that smile, because the two of them were half hanging out of the sleigh. They were so close to me that the Thief's long black braid was dangling right in front of my nose. I went to give it one last try to pull myself up, but before I could the Thief reached up, grabbed Mummy's gold tooth, and yanked it out of her mouth.

"You want to keep this tooth?" the Thief said, choking out the words. "Well, go *get* it!"

And she tossed it right out of the sleigh.

"My *toof*!" Mummy said. Unable to help herself, she lunged after it, right *over* the side of the sleigh!

Her upside-down face passed by mine, and then— just like that—she was gone.

No more Mummy.

I looked down to see if I could find her in the waves below.

Still a bad idea.

"A little help here!" I called, and the Thief held out her hand and hoisted me up into the sleigh.

"Nine for one," she said.

"And one for nine," I said.

Then I took control of the reins and turned the team back in the other direction, toward Isle X.

"On Dasher, on Dancer, on Prancer and Vixen!"

I mean, I *had* to say that, right?

EPILOGUE

So there you have it. The story of how the No-Good Nine saved Christmas!

Which is pretty ironic, when you think about it.

Santa found it more than ironic. In fact, he found it downright unbelievable. But give the guy credit—he stuck by what he had read out that morning, even the stuff he didn't want to. Namely, that no child would ever receive coal in their stocking again.

Yer welcome.

Santa would also be keeping his promises to the elves of Isle X. In this, he had no choice, because Lefty and Hendrick had formed a Union of Elfin Toy Makers, Local #1, to make sure that he did.

What's more, Santa gave us a sleigh and reindeer and told us to take them wherever we wanted to go.

That made up for every present he never gave us, and then some!

Our first stop was Quebec City, where the Truant

Officer delivered the Brothers Jack to the local Royal Canadian Mounted Police. As it wound up, the sonny-boys were wanted for plenty of crimes, and the Mounties were so impressed by the Truant Officer and his detailed journals that they offered him a job. As a real policeman!

Even if I still considered him my nemesis, I was happy for him.

As we got back into the sleigh, I realized that this was the first time the nine of us had ever been alone together. Y'know, without having to fear for our lives or anything.

"So, what do we do now?" Goody-Two-Shoes said.

We all looked at each other.

I've thought about this moment a lot in the many years since it happened, as it was a mighty BIG moment.

Under most circumstances, we would've gone our separate ways. But the thing was, we all liked being on a team. Mug Uglies aside, none us had ever even been in a club before. Heck, none of us had ever even had much in the way of *friends* before. (And you can probably see why.)

"Does anyone want to go home?" the Cruel said.

Not a one of us said yes.

"We have a magic sleigh, a flying reindeer, and a sack of Al Capone's cash . . ." the Thief said.

"We can go wherever we want and *do* whatever we want," the Brat said.

Everyone thought about it. Then

"What do y-y-y-**you** think we should do?"

It was *me* the Know-It-All was asking, and everyone turned to look in my direction.

I could tell you what I said—and what we *did*—but would you ever believe me?

THE END

JOHN BEMELMANS MARCIANO is the author of novels, chapter books, and picture books for young readers. His previous novel, *The Nine Lives of Alexander Baddenfield*, was illustrated by Sophie Blackall, with whom he also collaborated on the Witches of Benevento series. John continued the legacy of his grandfather, Ludwig Bemelmans, in *Madeline and the Cats of Rome*, *Madeline and the Old House in Paris*, *Madeline at the White House*, and *Madeline Says Merci*. He is also the author of two books for adults: *Anonyponymous* and *Whatever Happened to the Metric System?*

John lives in New Jersey, with his wife, Andromache, and their daughter, Galatea.